"Help! Help!" A.J. cried.

A log . . . a board . . . a branch . . . I had to find something. *Think, Satch, fast. A.J.'s drowning. Move!* I started to crawl out on the ice. A.J. seemed miles and miles away.

"No, Satch, no! You'll go through, too," Spinner screamed.

"There's no other way. Go for help, Spinner."

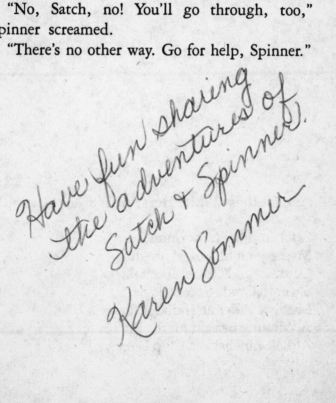

Have fun shareing the adventures of Satch & Spinner.

Karen Sommer

Ask for these White Horse titles from Chariot Books:

Satch and the Motormouth
Mystery on Mirror Mountain
Courage on Mirror Mountain
Seventh Grade Soccer Star
Mystery Rider at Thunder Ridge
A Winning Season for the Braves
At Left Linebacker, Chip Demory

NEW KID ON THE BLOCK

Karen Sommer

Chariot Books™
David C. Cook Publishing Co.

Dedicated to
"My Kids"
and
Thai tho son

蔡寿山

Chariot Books is an imprint of David C. Cook Publishing Co.
David C. Cook Publishing Co., Elgin, Illinois 60120
David C. Cook Publishing Co., Weston, Ontario

NEW KID ON THE BLOCK

Cover illustration by Ron Mazellan
Cover design by Stephen D. Smith

Third Printing, 1989
Printed in the United States of America
92 91 90 89 5 4 3

Library of Congress Cataloging-in-Publication Data
Sommer, Karen,
  New kid on the block.
  (A White horse book)
  Previously published as: Satch and the new kid, and: The new kid,
Spinner, and me.
  Summary: The arrival of a family of Vietnamese refugees sponsored by
eleven-year-old Satch's church requires him and his friends to make
many adjustments, with God's help.
  [1. Vietnamese Americans - Fiction. 2. Christian life - Fiction] I. Title.
PZ7.S6963Sb 1987 [Fic] 86-24323
ISBN 0-89191-746-2

Contents

1
Moving In

Brrrrrring! The phone rang.

"Hello?"

"Satch? You awake?"

"Yeah," I moaned, though I wasn't really awake.

"They're here!"

"Huh?"

"They're here. Come on down."

"Who's here?" I was waking up at last, but Spinner was still sounding crazy. Spinner's my best friend. He's famous for starting in the middle of a conversation. Usually, I could figure out what he meant, but he was making no sense whatever at 7:30

in the morning. "What are you talking about, Spinner?"

"The boat people. The refugee family. They're here!"

"Oh. You mean the family from Vietnam?" I asked.

"Who do you think I'm talking about? Tuna fishermen?" Spinner yelled into the phone. "Of course the Vietnamese family, you turkey. Wake up. Get over here, Satch, or you'll miss it."

"OK. OK. I'll hussle."

Spinner and I had been waiting since fifth grade for the arrival of the Vietnamese family. Our two churches were cosponsoring them. My mother and Mrs. Spinnelli were in charge of "Neighborhood Adjustment," because the new family was moving into the vacant house next to Spinner's. For over a year the churches had been renting that empty house. Each month we were told the homeless family would be arriving in a couple weeks. And each month there was the same disappointment—no family. It's never made any sense to me. There were thousands of homeless people, and we wanted to help just one little family and couldn't.

My mother just says, "That's the way the government works, Sidney. We have immigration laws to protect people, and sometimes the laws take so long to enact that innocent people get hurt." Mom was good at making something very simple turn into something confusing. Besides, what did Mom know? She was responsible for sticking me with a name like *Sidney*. The guys call me Satch. Sidney sounds like a sissy name. How could my parents have done such a nasty thing?

I grabbed my jeans and T-shirt. I flew into Mom's bedroom. "They're here. They're here," I shouted.

"What on earth are you talking about, Sidney Carlton?" My mother moaned from under the covers.

"The boat people. They're really here. Spinner just phoned. The family's moving in right now."

"Are you sure?" Mom was beginning to show signs of life. "I'd better call Ginny so we can get organized." Mom was in a trance, talking to herself.

"Gotta go. See ya."

Downstairs, I grabbed some toast and started for the door.

"Sid?" Mom called from upstairs.

"Yeah?" I was halfway out the door.

"Tell Ginny I'll call her."

"OK."

The door slammed behind me.

"And Sid?" Mom was calling out the window now.

"Yeah?"

"Don't make a pest of yourself at the new family's house."

Mom always said that. Hey, I was about to start sixth grade. I was eleven years old. I wasn't a baby anymore. Didn't she think I knew anything?

I raced to Spinner's house on my bike. Mrs. Spinnelli was in the kitchen clanking pans.

"Hi, Mrs. Spinnelli. Mom said she'd call."

"Thanks, Satch. Spinner's upstairs getting dressed. You can go on up."

Mrs. Spinnelli went right ahead with her clunking

9

and clanking. I flew upstairs two steps at a time.

"Spinner, I thought you'd be next door by now."

"I've been waiting for you. Besides, there's a pretty good view from up here. Look."

"How many of them are there? Any kids our age?" I was peering out the window now with Spinner.

"I can't tell, but there's a lot of them. Let's head over there now." Spinner finished tying his shoes.

We raced down the stairs and out the front door. Three or four cars were parked in front of Spinner's house. I recognized our minister, Reverend Miller.

"Satch Carlton, hello, sport," called Reverend Miller. "Come right over and meet our new family, the Lings."

"Hello, Mr. Miller. This is my best friend, Spinner. He lives next door. His family belongs to Redeemer Church."

"Howdy, Spinner." Reverend Miller smiled and shook Spinner's hand. He was always so friendly.

"How do you do, sir?" Spinner replied in his politest form.

"Well, boys, the Lings have a boy just about your age. How old are you fellas anyway?"

"Eleven," we both announced together.

"We're starting sixth grade next week," I added.

"Great! I bet you and Hai will become great friends." Reverend Miller looked pleased.

"Hi?" Spinner and I repeated together.

"You mean like the *hi* kind of hello?" I asked.

"Well, his name sounds like *hi*, but it's spelled H-a-i," Reverend Miller explained.

Spinner and I smiled at each other, wrinkling our

10

noses and eyebrows. We'd never heard such a strange name.

"Don't worry, fellas, he'll probably wonder about your names as much as you wonder about his. Remember, everything is strange for these people. Try to imagine yourself in a new place with strange food, strange clothes, and a strange language. The Ling family has been through some pretty rough times. I know I can count on you two men to make their adjustment as smooth as possible."

Reverend Miller walked Spinner and me toward the porch. Three frail-looking brown kids in scruffy clothes sat on the porch swing. The kids were trying out the new swing, speeding up and slowing down. Their hands and eyes were everywhere, inspecting the cushions, the hinges, and the armrests. When we stepped up onto the porch, they stopped immediately. They sunk down as if they'd done something wrong. The little girl peered out from underneath her eyebrows, afraid to look at us.

I wanted to tell the kids it was fine for them to swing. That's what a swing is for. Just looking at us seemed to terrify them, though. I tried to smile. They kept looking down at the ground.

Reverend Miller smiled that huge smile of his and said reassuringly, "It's OK. OK. You can swing." The kids seemed less nervous, but still cautious. The oldest boy put his head up now. The little girl kept looking through her eyebrows. The littlest one, I thought he was a boy, started fidgeting.

Mr. Miller kept smiling. He began introductions. "This is Satch. Saaaaaatch," he emphasized. "Eleven." Mr. Miller pointed to me and held up ten of his fingers and one of mine. "This is Spinner. Spiiiiinner. Eleven." Mr. Miller again held up ten of his fingers and grabbed one of Spinner's.

Spinner and I smiled. The kids still looked afraid of us.

"Satch," I repeated loudly. I pointed to myself. "Eleven," I said holding up ten of my fingers and borrowing one of Spinner's.

Spinner began to follow, "Spinner." He flashed his fingers, too. "Eleven."

At last, the older boy's expression started to change. Cautiously, he spoke very softly, "Saaaash?" He pointed to me.

Wow! Neato! He understood. "Yes, yes," I said shaking my head up and down and grinning so that every tooth showed.

The boy seemed braver. "Spinna?" the boy pointed to Spinner. Spinner flipped, too.

We asked, "You? Name?" We pointed to the boy, trying not to frighten him.

The boy's eyes lit up. They squinted as he spoke, "Hai." He pointed to himself. "*Muoi mot,*" he continued. He held up his ten fingers and one of his sister's.

Wow! He spoke Vietnamese. He must have said he's eleven, too. He was smaller than Spinner and me, but the eleven fingers must mean his age.

"Hai," Spinner and I repeated. We all grinned. Even the little girl had stopped looking out from under her eyebrows. The littlest one was wiggling around more now. The swing started to move again.

12

Hai pointed to his sister. "Mai" he announced. Holding up seven of her fingers, he said, "Bay."

"My," Spinner and I repeated. We were starting to get the hang of this now. Hai and Mai rhymed. It would be easy to remember their names.

The littlest boy next to Mai spoke up, "Jao." He held up three fingers.

"Chow," Spinner and I repeated, pointing to the wiggling little boy.

Jao's name would be easy to remember because I could think of food or "chow." Three years old, *hum*. Frankie Spinnelli was going to have company. Frankie was Spinner's pest of a little brother. Frankie was only three and a half, but he had already gotten into more trouble than most kids find in a lifetime.

"Jao," repeated the little fellow. He wanted us to keep saying his name.

"Chow, chow," Spinner and I kept repeating. All this chow stuff was making me hungry.

We went back to saying Hai's name and him saying ours. He wasn't pronouncing our names exactly right, but probably we were flubbing his name up, too, and he was polite enough not to correct us.

"Hey, wait here, I'll be right back," Spinner ordered as he took off toward his house. "I'll get Frankie." Usually, we tried to dart out of the house before Frankie could tail us. For once, Frankie might prove useful.

Reverend Miller stepped out of the house and onto the porch again. "Well, I see you've made friends already," he grinned. We all smiled up at him.

Behind Mr. Miller came a horde of people. I think some of them were from Spinner's church. Finally, the rest of the Vietnamese family stepped out. They smiled and nodded and smiled and nodded. With their heads bobbing up and down it looked like waves rolling back and forth across the beach.

Mr. Miller started pointing and introducing people. "Lee, Sue, Kim, Moc . . ." I was losing track, and he wasn't even halfway done. There was a mother, father, two older sisters, maybe a grandmother, a baby, and of course the three kids we'd already met. Nine people altogether. Wow. That's a big family. I'd hate to have to do the dishes in their family. They kept nodding and smiling as they were introduced. It was making me seasick.

Surprisingly, the father spoke some English, "Nice, nice." He nodded. His voice sounded strange, almost like a whisper. Pretty soon, I realized I was nodding and smiling, too. This was contagious. No wonder I felt seasick.

Spinner rounded the corner juggling four ice-cream cones. Frankie was with him carrying two more.

"Spinna," announced Hai to his family. He was really catching on fast. His family bowed again.

Spinner passed out the ice-cream cones to us kids. Hai, Mai, and Jao watched Spinner, Frankie, and me. Spinner and I licked with long, exaggerated tongue movements. Frankie just lapped away as usual, making a chocolate mess all over his face.

"Ice cream, *ummmmmm*," I said, rubbing my tummy.

"Ice cream, *ummmmmm*," Spinner licked and patted

his stomach, too.

Jao started licking. Hai and Mai looked at their cones and then at their father.

"*Con Có thẽ ăn*," he said. I guess he said they could eat them, because Hai and Mai began to lick their cones.

"I creeeeem," Hai repeated after three or four large licks. "*Tot.*" I think he meant "good," because he was smiling and rubbing his tummy, too.

"Ice cream, toe," I echoed back to Hai. It was kind of neat to learn some Vietnamese.

Mai soon was brave enough to join in, "I cream. *Tot.*"

Jao was too busy eating the ice cream to take time out for any words. He and Frankie Spinnelli looked like a pair of melted chocolate igloos.

Hai, Spinner, and I licked and *ummed* and *ummed* and licked. We couldn't stop watching each other and smiling back and forth between swallows. I knew we had done more than just share ice cream. We'd made some pretty scared kids welcome in a new home in Michigan. That felt even better than eating ice cream at nine o'clock in the morning.

2
Cherries Jubilee

All the neighbor ladies, Mom and Mrs. Spinnelli included, were busy cooking everything they could find for the new family. Spinner and I were always making trips to the Min-a-Mart. Today, Mom needed celery and carrots for soup and more flour for pies. She never made *us* that many pies! Going to the store wasn't all bad, though. Usually, I could weasel the extra change out of Mom and buy a goody.

"Keep the change?" I asked.

"I suppose, but *no candy.* You've had enough!"

"Aw, Mom, look at these muscles. They're not suffering."

"You heard me. If you want something sweet, buy some fruit. What about raisins? At least they're good for you. Do you understand?"

"Yeah, yeah. OK." I relented. Mom was warming up for her nutrition act. No sense arguing with her. In no time flat, she'd have me backed into a corner, and I'd never see so much as a potato chip for a month.

Spinner and I rode our bikes the few blocks to the store.

"What do ya think our new teacher will be like?" Spinner asked. School was only three days away. We were always anxious to see the gang again, but breaking in a new teacher every year was murder.

We parked our bikes outside the store. "Let's see, flour's probably in this aisle." I walked down the third row, checking out the cake mixes, chocolate chips, and all that good stuff. The emphatic *no candy* was ringing in my ears. I grabbed a bag of flour. We drifted over to the vegetables. Spinner picked up the celery and carrots.

"You gonna get some fruit like your mom said?"

"Yuck!"

"Yeah, I know, my mom thinks an apple is something to rave about. And pears. She goes absolutely crazy over those free pears on the tree in the backyard."

"Well, let's see what there is." The grapes looked fair. The bananas looked sick.

"Satch, over here. Look." Spinner was pointing to a sign: Washed Black Sweet Cherries.

We each tasted one. "Yum!" They were so sweet,

it was like eating candy. The fruit idea didn't seem so bad.

We picked up a quart of the cherries and high-tailed it for the checkout counter.

After delivering the groceries to my house, we headed for Spinner's porch with the cherries in hand.

"Sidney?" Mom called after us. "Don't bother the Lings. Let them have a few days of rest. They've had a long and sleepless journey."

"We're not gonna bug 'em, Mom. Can't we even watch from Spinner's house? Maybe the kids will wanta play."

"If they're outside, OK. If they're inside, though, don't go ringing their doorbell. The baby might be asleep, and they probably would like a little privacy after these first days of confusion."

"OK. OK." Mothers! They think kids have mush between their ears. We weren't gonna bother anyone.

Spinner and I sat on his front porch, ready to dive into the cherries. As soon as I plopped the first cherry into my mouth, who should appear? That pesky little brother of Spinner's, Frankie the Freeloader.

Frankie could smell food a mile away, especially *good* food. No one could get him to sit at a meal, but when dessert arrived, he always popped up out of nowhere. If the FBI could only harness that nose of Frankie's, they could sniff out hundreds of crooks. After Frankie sniffed the criminals out, they'd probably beg to be put in jail, just to escape the little monster.

"Gimme, gimme," whined Frankie.

"All right! But don't make a pig out of yourself,"

Spinner warned.

There was no use trying to keep the cherries from Frankie. I knew from past experience Frankie always whined until he got his way. Mrs. Spinnelli would inevitably appear at the door and give Spinner her share-or-else lecture. Frankie the Freeloader always got what he wanted.

Fortunately, Frankie lost interest in the cherries when Hai and Jao stepped out on their front porch. Neato! We motioned the two of them to come over as we jumped over the porch railing. The five of us met on the sidewalk.

"Hi, Hai," I said, waving a greeting. It sounded as if I was stuttering.

"Hi," Hai returned the greeting.

Everyone grinned, not knowing just where to go with this big conversation. I held out the box of cherries. "Toe," I said, trying to remember if my first Vietnamese word sounded like it was supposed to. Silence. *Hmm.* Maybe toe doesn't mean good after all.

I took a cherry. "Cherries, good." I tried to look pleased. The cherries were good, but I guess I was overacting.

Spinner took a cherry and repeated the charade. His acting was worse than mine.

Bravely, Hai followed our lead. "Shareeze." He smiled. Hai chewed and spit out the pit onto the sidewalk. "OK. Good."

We were just getting serious about eating the cherries when Mrs. Spinnelli came out the door. She politely greeted everyone and then announced, "I'm going to Satch's house for a few minutes. Sara Jane and I need to get these menus coordinated. Spinner, you'll have to watch Frankie.

"*Aw*, Mom," groaned Spinner.

"Now, enough of that. I'll only be gone about fifteen minutes."

Mrs. Spinelli bent down and kissed Frankie, saying, "Be good, honey. I have to go to Satch's house a few minutes."

"Me, too. Me, too, Mommy," Frankie pleaded.

"No, not this time. I'll just be gone a little while."

Frankie wasn't going to let Mrs. Spinnelli off that easily. "I wanta go, too. Me, too." Frankie was just starting to warm up.

"You can play with Jao, Frankie. Think how much fun you'll have in the sandbox." Mrs. Spinnelli had outmanuvered him. She kissed Frankie again and quickly walked down the porch steps.

"Bye-bye, Mommy." Frankie tried to wave sadly. But no sooner did Mrs. Spinnelli turn her back than Frankie grabbed Jao and headed for the backyard.

"Should we follow them?" I asked suspiciously.

"Naw, there's just that old sandbox back there. The yard's all fenced in. They can't go anywhere," Spinner said confidently.

Hai, Spinner, and I went back to chomping on the cherries. The sidewalk was beginning to look like it had the measles. There were cherry pits everywhere. Chew. Spit. Swallow. Chew. Spit. Swallow. The cherries were so sweet, they just slid down our throats.

Hai spit a pit out about three feet. Then I spit a pit out farther. Spinner shot one out at least five feet.

Pretty soon, we were having a contest, cheering every time one of us beat the old record.

"*Poo*," I shot one pit out past Spinner's pit.

"*Poo*," Hai landed one out beyond mine.

"Yea!" Spinner and I cheered for Hai. We patted him on the back.

"Watch this," said Spinner confidently. "*Poo*," he shot out the cherry pit. It missed Hai's last shot by just inches. Hai and I laughed. Spinner gritted his teeth and squinted his eyes. He threw his fist at the air, pretending to be mad.

The three of us had just about emptied the quart of cherries and redecorated the sidewalk when I heard Frankie call from down the driveway.

"Pinner. Pinner. Look at me. Jack and the Beantalk. *Wheee*." We all turned around. My heart sank between my feet. My feet were glued to the cement.

"Oh, no!" shrieked Spinner.

Hai gasped. Then he muttered something in Vietnamese.

Frankie had really done it this time.

Frankie and Jao were on the garage roof throwing pears and sand. They pranced and danced up there as if they were having a party. They thought they'd really done something cool. Really cool, all right. They were about ready to break their necks. The next thing they'd probably try would be flying.

"DON'T MOVE! STAY THERE! YOU HEAR ME! YOU STAY RIGHT THERE, OR I'LL KILL YOU!" Spinner screamed. Either way, Frankie was gonna get pulverized.

Spinner was running down the driveway in a

frenzy. Hai and I followed.

"*Chet rot*," Hai shouted at Jao. I didn't need a translation. Jao was gonna get pulverized, too.

"Help me with this," Spinner yelled from inside the garage. He was trying to lift the ladder off the garage wall. It was really heavy and clumsy to handle.

"Mom will skin me alive if she finds out Frankie is on the garage roof. That rattlesnake. How does he think of so many ways to find trouble?"

"How did they get up there?" I asked, holding one end of the ladder.

"Frankie probably climbed up the pear tree. He's half monkey, ya' know."

I know. We stood the stepladder up beside the garage. It was too short. Frankie and Jao didn't seem to mind. They were loving all this attention.

"Pinner can't catch Frank-o." Frankie was sing-songing away, trying to tease Spinner and me. He danced a little. He dropped pears on the driveway. He sifted sand into Spinner's face.

"Knock it off, you creep. Now stand still." Spinner kept screaming at Frankie while he climbed up the ladder. The ladder was definitely not the answer.

"*Chet rot*," Hai yelled, shaking his fist in the air.

Spinner was too upset to think straight. The ladder was too short. I had to come up with a solution.

"I'll climb up the pear tree and onto the roof. Then I'll lower Frankie and Jao to you on the ladder," I ordered.

"Yeah, that ought to do it," answered Spinner, deep in thought. I motioned Hai to steady the ladder.

22

I started up the pear tree. Frankie and Jao were giggling and jumping up and down. Thank heavens, they'd run out of pears and sand to throw.

"All right, you clowns, stand still," I screamed. How could they think this was just a game? It was a long way down. If they fell, they'd surely break at least ten or fifteen bones—if they didn't crack their skulls first.

Frankie started jumping up and down in real excitement. "Mommy, Mommy, see me. I'm Jack and the Bean-talk."

Oh, no, that was all we needed. My stomach turned around a few times. Mrs. Spinnelli was running down the driveway, panic-stricken. Her mouth and eyes were open so wide, the rest of her face was hidden.

"Frankie, my baby! My baby! What on earth are you doing up there?" she shrieked.

I jumped onto the roof. "Don't worry, Mrs. Spinnelli. They just got to playing and got carried away. I'll get them down." I was trying to sound calm in the face of danger.

Mrs. Spinnelli didn't fall for it. She kept on ranting and raving, "A little carried away, you say. They could get killed up there. Oh, my poor, poor baby. Be careful, honey. Mommy's here. Don't be afraid."

Afraid? Frankie Spinnelli wasn't afraid of *anything*. I was the one who was terrorized.

Mrs. Spinnelli was still freaking out. Hai scooted up the pear tree and onto the roof. Mrs. Spinnelli steadied the ladder for Spinner. I was glad Hai joined me. This was a much tougher job from up top than it looked like from down below. Hai and I lowered Jao down to Spinner on the ladder. Spinner carried him step by step down the ladder to the ground.

Mrs. Spinnelli couldn't wait for Spinner to climb back up the ladder for Frankie. She climbed the ladder herself. She was seconds away from a heart attack. Hai and I lowered Frankie. Mrs. Spinnelli grabbed him desperately. She hugged and kissed him all over, crying throughout it all, "My baby, thank God. My poor little baby." Mrs. Spinnelli did that for about five minutes.

Then Mrs. Spinnelli turned to Spinner and me with fire in her eyes. "How did this happen? I leave you in charge for fifteen minutes—*Fifteen little minutes*—and this happens. You two should be old enough to watch one defenseless three-year-old. . . ."

Defenseless? Frankie? Never.

"Mom, we were out front. We thought—"

"You thought? You thought you'd just forget about your brother's safety? An eleven-year-old boy ought to take more responsibility."

My mother gives me that same lecture, too. Responsibility. It only works when they want it to work.

Mrs. Spinnelli was still sputtering away, "And you two clean up those cherry pits all over the sidewalk, before you, Anthony Spinnelli, spend the rest of the afternoon in your room."

With that, Mrs. Spinnelli stormed into the house, carrying Frankie in her arms and mumbling, "Thank God, my baby. Thank God, my baby. . . ."

Frankie thought the whole incident was great. He waved at us as he peered over his mother's shoulder. He'd zapped us again, and he knew it.

Hai slipped away home after the three of us swept up the cherry pits. It's a good thing Mrs. Spinnelli didn't see the smashed pears in the driveway and sand in the eaves troughs. We would have been blamed for that, too.

Spinner and I had taught Hai some pretty important American lessons:

1. Never spit cherry pits on the sidewalks.
2. Never trust Frankie Spinnelli.
3. Never eat too many cherries at one time. An hour later diarrhea takes hold.

3
Opening Day
Jitters

Wednesday arrived. Spinner and I headed down
Oliver Street toward Roosevelt School. "My mom
says our teacher is young," Spinner announced.

"Decent. How does your mom know?"

"She saw The Turtle's wife in the grocery store."

The Turtle was the school principal, Sylvester
Tuttle. He had a special way of sticking his neck out
to peer into a noisy classroom if the teacher wasn't
there. The Turtle would pull his neck back into his
shell when the kids quieted back down. He never said
a word. He just plodded down the hallway slow and
steady looking for the next noisy classroom.

"Hey, there's Pete and A.J. dead ahead," Spinner yelled.

Pete and A.J. were our best buddies. Mr. Spinnelli called us the Fearsome Foursome. Mr. Spinnelli knew how crazy the four of us could act. He was our coach during the fall soccer season.

"*Aaaay,* you turkeys. Wait up."

Pete and A.J. stopped and turned around.

"What's the scoop?" A.J. asked. "Have you got any dope on the new teach?"

Spinner started, "Well, she's supposed to be young. I think this is her first job."

"Really?" A.J. spoke up. "Boy, are we gonna make her grow old."

I almost felt sorry for our new teacher. She didn't stand a chance against the Fearsome Foursome. By sixth grade, we had our strategy perfected.

"Have you guys heard about Hai, the new Vietnamese kid?" I asked.

"Hi who? Sounds like he doesn't know whether he's coming or going," A.J. jeered. He started prancing around acting silly. He put his fingers to the edge of his eyes, pulling the skin to make his eyes look Chinese. To top it off, he pretended to have buckteeth.

That was sure a creepy thing to do. I half grinned like the others, but I wasn't enjoying A.J.'s performance. What was A.J. trying to prove?

"Well, have you met him?" I went on. "He's our age and might be in our class. He's kinda—"

"Hey, knock it off. He isn't worth the fuss," A.J. interrupted.

"Yeah," Pete chimed in. "Let's decide what we're gonna do to the girls to make 'em scream or something. How about that plastic tarantula you got up north, A.J.?"

The three of them started making plans as to whose chair they'd set the tarantula on. I couldn't stop thinking about A.J.'s bucktooth Chinaman act. What did he have against Hai? Was he afraid the Fearsome Foursome might get split up? That was impossible. We were invincible. We were a team. Being nice to a kid who didn't know anything about living in America or speaking English wouldn't split up our friendship.

The four of us filed into the classroom. WOW! There she was. Our teacher. She was young, all right, and that wasn't all. She was a real knockout.

The room was absolutely silent, even eerie. It's not natural for twenty-nine kids to be that quiet. All of us were totally occupied watching this blonde creature's every movement.

"Good morning, class. My name is Miss Hepburn." She wrote her name on the board. "I'd like to get to know you, and I'd like you to get to know me." She walked toward A.J. He kept swallowing every two seconds. I thought he was gonna choke on his tongue.

"Perhaps, we can introduce ourselves to get better acquainted," she continued. She started coming my way. I tried to look cool, but I was getting goose bumps, and my left eye started twitching. I didn't want her to think I was doing something dumb like winking at her, but that crazy eyelid just wouldn't stop twitching. I rubbed it. It twitched harder. I rubbed harder.

"Have you something in your eye?" Miss Hepburn leaned toward me.

"Oh, no, no," I blurted out, turning my head to the side.

"It looks so red, and you were rubbing it so hard," Miss Hepburn pursued.

"Just a little itch. It's OK." I tried to cover up. What embarrassment.

"Well, to continue, I'm originally from . . ." She kept on talking. My eyelid was still going berserk. I think it was sending out Morse code or something.

"Now who'd like to volunteer to tell me something about himself? I'd like to get to know you as quickly as possible."

A grimy hand waved in the air practically pulling the body attached to it out of her seat. The class loudmouth, better known as Motormouth Marcie, was volunteering. She could talk on any subject. And her favorite subject was Marcie. I could see it coming. We'd be here all day, and Marcie's motor would be going strong right up until the last bell.

"My name is Marcie Cook. I'm eleven. I have one little sister, Mandy. She's five and starting kindergarten today. I went to Disney World last summer. I have a cat named Samantha, Sam for short. I'm good at reading. I like . . ." Blah, blah, blah. Marcie wasn't good at reading. She wasn't good at anything, except running her mouth and saying nothing.

"Could we have another volunteer?"

Girls kept talking . . . and talking . . . and talking.

Then Miss Hepburn started to call on some guys. My knees shook. I knew she was gonna pick me soon. My eye would probably pop right out of my head, and the whole class would roll over in hysterics.

Whew! She called on A.J. "*Uh*, I'm Alex Jackson, better known as A.J. I have two older brothers. One is in high school. The other one's . . . well, he's not around here. I play goalie. . . ."

I didn't know A.J. had *two* brothers. He never mentioned more than one.

Miss Hepburn looked down at me. Gulp. I slowly stood up. "My name is Satch Carlton. Well, really my name is Sidney Carlton the third, but with a name like that a guy just has to have a nickname." My eye had finally stopped twitching. Instead my knees were quivering. I wanted to look down to see if my pants were running a race without my feet. "My favorite subjects are math and science." That ought to impress her. "I have two older sisters." I didn't know whether or not to mention that Mom and Dad were divorced. Better not. I slid back into my seat.

Knock. Knock.

The Turtle was at the door. Beside him was a shadow. It was Hai.

"Excuse me, Miss Hepburn. I would like to introduce a very new and special student to you and to the class." Mr. Tuttle stepped into the room.

Hai hovered beside him. He looked even more terrified than the first day we'd met on the porch. Poor kid. I wouldn't like to be standing up there with twenty-nine sets of eyes bugging out at me, either.

"Students, this is Hai Ling," Mr. Tuttle continued. Hai nodded when he heard his name. "Hai and his family are from Vietnam. They speak no English yet. I know you will make Hai and his family welcome."

"Thank you, Mr. Tuttle," Miss Hepburn said, approaching Hai. "Welcome." She smiled. Hai bowed and looked at the floor. "Does anyone here already know Hai?"

Spinner and I waved our hands simultaneously. Hai's sick expression changed to one of relief. He smiled. He looked alive, finally.

"Let's give Hai a seat near someone he's comfortable with," Miss Hepburn announced. "Marcie, could we move you over to the empty seat in the first row?"

Amazing! Marcie was speechless. Her motor stalled. What could she say? Marcie trudged over to her new seat.

What a stroke of luck: Hai was between Spinner and me, and Motormouth Marcie was four rows away.

4
Kickball
Language

Recess was fast approaching. "What game might you play at recess that's easy enough for Hai to understand?" Miss Hepburn asked. "He's going to learn most of our language from you and the activities you involve him in. I know you'll all do your best to be tolerant and understanding."

"What about kickball?" suggested Spinner. "Yeah!" echoed half the kids.

"That sounds like a very good idea." Miss Hepburn chose Spinner and Pete. Rats! It was more fun when the Fearsome Foursome were together.

Spinner and Pete stood up at opposite sides of the

room. "Spinner, you may start with the first pick."

"Satch Carlton," called Spinner.

I walked over to Spinner and stood beside him. Pete was bound to pick A.J.

Spinner whispered to me, "Should we go for Hai?"

I nodded approval.

"Hai Ling," Spinner announced.

We motioned Hai to come join us. Hai cautiously got out of his seat and stood beside us.

A.J. glared across the room at our team as Pete and Spinner continued to choose sides. Why was A.J. staring at Hai so hard? Guess he was just sizing up our team.

Each team now had fifteen members. We headed for the playground. Now, how to explain the game to Hai? I put the ball on the ground and pretended to kick it with my foot.

"Kick," I stressed.

"Keek," Hai mimicked. Close enough.

Our team was playing in the field first. Spinner was the pitcher. Hai and I covered second base.

Pete came up to kick first. He popped up the ball to Spinner's waiting arms. "Out!" One away. Our team cheered.

Now A.J. was up. He hit a high fly way out into left field. A girl tried to catch it, but she chickened out at the last moment and covered her head with her arms. The ball dropped to the ground and rolled farther into the outfield. She chased the ball and heaved it to me just as A.J. was heading for second base. Oh, no. Hai was standing on the invisible baseline—right in A.J.'s path. Hai was going to get creamed. A.J. was charging toward second base just as I caught the ball. Hai tried to scoot out of the way by moving sideways. That was just the direction A.J. was taking to try to run around Hai. *Smack! Plop!* They collided and landed in a heap at my feet.

"Out!" I yelled, as I tagged A.J. with the ball. I helped Hai to his feet. I was sure he didn't have the slightest idea what this game was all about.

"Out, my eye! That creep was standing on the baseline!" screamed A.J.

"Come on, A.J. You know you would have been out even if Hai hadn't been there. Besides, you can't expect Hai to know all the rules."

A.J. wasn't budging. "If you're gonna play kickball, then play by the rules. Why should everything be special for *him?*"

Why was A.J. going looney-tooney? He knew he would have been out anyway. He knew Miss Hepburn said to help Hai. He knew Hai hadn't done anything on purpose. I could see Hai out of the corner of my eye. He knew we were arguing about him. I was afraid A.J. would break out in his bucktooth Chinaman act. I couldn't let Hai see that. He might think we all hated him.

"OK. OK. Take second base and *shut up!*" I yelled.

I motioned Hai off the baseline, and the game continued. The first half of the inning ended with Pete's team ahead: 5-0.

Our team came up to kick. Spinner was first. Great. A line drive between first and second. Base hit. We decided to let Hai kick before we had too many outs. Pete rolled the ball toward Hai. *Boom!*

The ball rose into the air over the head of the second baseman. I had the feeling Hai wouldn't need any more kickball lessons from me. He streaked to first base.

A.J. ran to get under the fly ball. *Please don't catch it, A.J. Let Hai get a hit.* Marcie was out in the field craning her neck to see the ball. Her motor was running as usual. "I'll get it. I'll get it." *Clunk!* She banged into A.J. *Thanks, Marcie.* For once, she came in handy. Hai stopped at second base.

Spinner poured on the speed for home plate, taking advantage of the confussion between Marcie and A.J.

"Home it. Home it." The catcher was jumping up and down on home plate, trying to get A.J.'s attention.

A.J. recovered his footing, grabbed the ball, and heaved it toward the catcher. Terrible throw. The catcher had to run out ten feet from the plate. Spinner scored. "Yea!" Our team went into jubilation. We had our first run and no outs.

"Hey, look you guys," pointed Spinner. "Hai's on third base." Our team had been so busy cheering Spinner home that we'd forgotten about motioning Hai to third. He'd figured it out all by himself. Hai was in scoring position, ready to run with the next pitch. What a natural.

A girl stepped up to the plate. She kicked a pop fly out to A.J. This time A.J. was ready for Marcie. "Get out of here, you birdbrain. I'll cream you if you so much as breathe near this ball." Marcie backed off. I almost think A.J. was serious. The look on his face was getting meaner and meaner. A.J. caught the fly.

Out. One away.

Suddenly Hai started running for home, having tagged third after A.J.'s catch. Hai knew exactly what to do.

"Send it home. He's gonna score," screamed Pete from the pitcher's mound.

A.J. threw the ball at Hai. *Whizzzz*. It was right on target. Hai was gonna be out. He leaped three feet into the air. The ball magically sailed under his feet. Hai sped across home plate for the run. A.J. glared in disgust.

Our whole team surrounded Hai. We hugged and cheered. The huddle almost smothered Hai. We were so happy he had scored, but I felt something more. It wasn't the point that mattered. Hai could talk now. Hai could talk in kickball language.

5
Getting in Condition

For a first-year teacher Miss Hepburn seemed very experienced at making tough assignments. On the board she wrote: Due Monday—Three Personal Accomplishments I Hope to Achieve This Semester.

This definitely was no true-or-false quickie. The first week of school, and already we were expected to *think*.

Naturally Motormouth Marcie was waving her hand like a flag flapping in fifty-mile-an-hour wind, "Miss Hepburn, do these accomplishments have to be about school?"

"No, they are *not* to be about school," Miss

Hepburn explained. "I want you to examine other areas of your life. School is just one part of it. What about family? friends? church? activities? Really look deeply. Where do you want to be in January?"

I never really thought about what I *wanted* to achieve. Teachers usually told you what you *had* to achieve, or else. This could be interesting.

Spinner questioned, "Are you going to read these lists out loud to the class?"

"No. This will be a confidential matter. I will try to discuss your goals with each of you privately. At the end of the semester you will evaluate your progress."

Heavy. This was gonna be a huge project, examining my whole life.

"Are we gonna be graded on this?" A.J. spoke up.

"No, you will not be given a letter grade." A sigh of relief swept the classroom. Miss Hepburn continued, "That doesn't diminish the importance of this project. It simply means that personal goals cannot be measured by letter grades. You, and only you, will evaluate what is important and what you have learned by setting goals for yourself." She paused a few seconds. "Really think."

Wow. Miss Hepburn was like no other teacher I'd ever come across. She wanted something special from each of us. And it wasn't just fifty math problems. This thinking stuff was a whole new ball game. It might be fun. I never seriously looked that far into the future. Where do I want my life to be in January?

This weekend my sisters and I would be at Dad's. Maybe he would have some ideas.

Saturday arrived and so did Dad. Lately he was on a running craze.

"Come and run with me, Satch," coaxed Dad.

How was I gonna worm out of this one?

"It's great exercise. It builds up your heart muscle, Satch."

Why in the world would I want an oversized heart muscle? Arms maybe. Legs possibly. But how does one flex a heart?

"You'll really feel in shape, sport. You'll be in great condition for soccer." Dad went on and on.

No thanks. I'd rather stay exactly like I am, a ninety-nine-pound weakling.

"You'll feel terrific when we're done," Dad was putting on his shoes and not about to let up on me. Running had taught him one thing, determination.

"OK. OK," I relented.

We headed to Emerson Park.

"So how's school this year, tiger?" Dad started.

"Pretty good, I guess."

"How's your teacher?"

"She's young. This is her first year. She's really a knockout, Dad."

"Oh? So you're noticing those things now?"

"Well, sort of. I think she's gonna be neat besides that, though. She's heavy into thinking, Dad."

"Thinking? Come again?"

I explained about setting goals as we jogged. Dad and I were bouncing up and down, and sometimes the words came out of me with big blobs of air in them. They sounded strange, but Dad was getting the idea.

"Any possibilities?" Dad asked.

"Actually, I'm kinda stuck. I sure would like to see our soccer team win the league championship. Do you think that's a good goal?"

"Sounds great to me," Dad panted. "Your team came mighty close last season. Can't hurt to try."

We jogged on. I had to stop talking for a while. It was taking too much energy. I never realized it was so difficult to keep my mouth and feet going at the same time.

"How's the Fearsome Foursome?" Dad puffed.

"Terrific." Then I remembered A.J. Was the Fearsome Foursome OK? Was Hai a problem?

"Hey, Dad," I took in a deep breath, "we have a new kid from Vietnam in our room. His name is Hai. He's part of the refugee family brought here by the church. Remember?"

"Yeah."

"Hai's great at sports. He's really a regular guy. You should see him play kickball. Mr. Spinnelli is gonna try to get him on our soccer team."

We turned right, bobbing up and down in rhythm. I was sure my feet were crunched into my ankles by now.

"Maybe he'll be just the added touch to help you win the league championship." Dad grabbed his breath. "I'm glad you're helping the new boy. I hear that the family has been homeless for years."

I stopped to collect some much-needed energy. I flopped down on the grass at the edge of Emerson Park.

Homeless? For years? That's incredible.

"But, Dad, where did the Lings live if they were homeless?"

"Well, I don't know all the answers. The information the churches received was pretty sketchy. The family can't explain things because they don't speak enough English, and no one here in Owosso speaks much Vietnamese. Their records just show the Asian cities where they've lived. It's pretty hard for us to understand living in the midst of war."

My mind flashed to war. Bombs exploding. Buildings dropping. Suddenly, I saw Hai's face. His family was caught in the middle of soldiers, guns, and bodies. My stomach turned over a couple times. *God, how could you let that happen?*

Dad stood up, "Well, Satch, I'm glad to see the Fearsome Foursome is on the right track. You're helping the new boy. You're making the effort. I'm proud to see you guys care."

Did we? I guess we did. Well, at least I knew I did, but I wasn't so sure about Pete and A.J.— especially A.J. Something strange between Hai and A.J. was going on. I couldn't explain it.

I picked up my limp body. We headed for Dad's apartment. All this blood pumping around from my bulging heart was making my brain work overtime. But I was better off thinking about Hai and A.J. than feeling my feet pound directly into my knees.

Why was A.J. gunning for Hai? A.J. never even met Hai until school started. Was he just fooling around with his bucktooth Chinaman act? Why did A.J. stare at Hai? Did Hai really look that different?

"Dad, what makes a person dislike someone else

before they even know each other?"

"I couldn't give *one* reason, Satch. People do a lot of strange things sometimes to hide their true feelings."

Maybe Dad has something there. Is A.J. hiding something behind that class clown act?

"But what could make someone want to hide his feelings?" I asked.

Dad looked confused now. He hated talking in generalities. I was going to have to expose A.J.

"It's like this, Dad. A.J. doesn't like Hai. But he decided he didn't like Hai before they ever met. A.J.'s acting like a bully. Why?"

"Maybe this tough-guy approach of A.J.'s is really a cover-up. Maybe A.J.'s a little afraid of Hai," Dad theorized.

"Afraid of Hai? Hai wouldn't beat anyone up."

"I don't mean afraid of what Hai can do to him physically. He might be afraid of having you pay more attention to Hai than to him. Understand?"

"Kinda . . ." Maybe Dad was right. Maybe A.J. thought the Fearsome Foursome would split up.

We were almost back to Dad's apartment. I was exhausted.

"Dad, what should I do about A.J.? I don't think he'll give Hai a chance."

"Well, don't be too hard on A.J. Include both of them in your activities. He'll come around. Give him time."

"I hope so. I'd hate to have to choose between them."

I was dragging my feet up the steps. As far as

being in shape, we both looked like our shape had been crushed by a garbage truck. We smelled like it, too.

Dad was right about one thing, though. I felt terrific. My body was completely wiped out, but my thoughts were spinning. Without realizing it, I had two goals for Miss Hepburn's assignment: winning the soccer championship and helping Hai find a new home in America. At least my brain was getting in condition.

6
English Lessons

On Monday I turned in my three goals. I decided my third accomplishment would be earning enough money to buy a new dirt bike, like the ones shown in *Sports Illustrated*. Mom and Dad were united on that subject. If I wanted a new bike, I'd have to pay for it. My old bike was "plenty good enough." What do parents know about dirt biking anyway?

On Tuesday Miss Hepburn called me up to her desk. "Hi, Satch."

She was holding my assignment. Oh, no. I could see it coming. It wasn't right.

Her eyes left the paper and came up to me. "Looks

like some fine goals here, Satch. You're a pretty good soccer player?"

"Yeah, I guess so," I mumbled. I'd never had a teacher who cared about my soccer ability. She was certainly different.

"I see your second goal is helping Hai. That's a very good idea. Would you like to be Hai's tutor?"

"Tutor? What's that?"

"It's like being Hai's own personal teacher."

"Yeah, that could be neat. What would I do?"

"For starters, you two could push your desks together. Hai could learn from you by looking at your paper."

"You mean he could copy? It would be legal?"

Miss Hepburn smiled and half laughed. "Yes, Satch, it would be legal. All we really want to do is help Hai."

Wow. Sixth grade was great. Miss Hepburn was really something for a first-year teacher. I sure hope she never gets old.

Hai went to first grade for reading with his sister and a special teacher's aid. But the rest of the time he was in our room, right beside me.

On Wednesday Miss Hepburn started reviewing fractions. I don't know any kid alive who ever liked fractions. My older sisters still complain about them. I copied the first problem from the board on my paper. I motioned to Hai to copy it, too. I watched him start to write. Good. Numbers at least look the same in Vietnamese.

Miss Hepburn was using some fancy words like denominators and numerators. I never could keep them straight. What she was doing was changing one-half to four-eighths so she could add the fractions. Hai sat attentively, but I was sure he didn't have the slightest idea what she was saying. I pointed to my paper and wrote: $\frac{1}{8} + \frac{1}{2} = \frac{1}{8} + \frac{4}{8} = \frac{5}{8}$

"See?" I whispered.

Hai grinned. He slid his paper across my desk. "See?" he echoed.

My jaw fell open. Hai had solved the problem when he copied it from the board. What a calculator he had up there in his brain. He didn't even have to change one-half to four-eighths first. He had figured out the whole thing in his head.

After a few more examples, Miss Hepburn started a math game. She called the leader in each row to the chalkboard. She read a problem out loud. The first person to correctly solve the problem at the board scored a point for his or her row. Cheers went up every time a point was awarded. Finally the game got to the last person in each row. Hai and I headed for the board along with the other four competitors. Oh, oh. That meant A.J. He sat in the last seat in the row against the windows. A.J. strutted to the board trying to be Mr. Cool. He was a whiz at math, and he knew it.

The six of us took our places at the board. Miss Hepburn announced, "one-fourth plus three-sixteenths." I wrote it on the board. Hai started copying his own problem after he read mine. Without hesitation, Hai wrote 7/ .

Suddenly A.J. announced, "Done. Seven-sixteenths."

A.J.'s row cheered. A.J. bowed as if he knew he could skunk us all.

Then it occurred to me. Hai really knew the answer first. He just didn't have the same chance. Not knowing the English words for the numbers, he had to see the problem before he could write it down. Everyone else was working the problem by then.

I raised my hand. "Miss Hepburn, could someone write the problem on the board for Hai when you say it? He has to copy the problem when the rest of us are all set to solve it."

"Good idea, Satch," Miss Hepburn agreed. A girl from Hai's row was appointed to write Hai's problem while Miss Hepburn dictated.

"OK, ready?" Miss Hepburn continued. "Three-fourths minus two-eighths."

Seconds ticked away. A.J. was busy scrambling numerators and denominators. The chalk was flying.

Hai tapped me on the shoulder. "Doon. OK?"

"Yes. Done. Great."

Miss Hepburn led the applause. The whole class was stunned.

I gave Hai a pat on the back. I knew that calculator brain of his could do it.

Miss Hepburn called out four more problems. Each time Hai followed with, "Doon?" Each time he had it right. Even the kids in the losing rows were cheering Hai. Everyone was really happy for Hai. Everyone that is, except A.J. Each time we turned to the board to write another problem, I could hear A.J. mumbling under his breath. He wasn't mumbling about lousy fractions. It was more than that. A.J. glared at

Hai. I didn't like the side of A.J. I was beginning to see. Something was eating away at the old A.J.

On Thursday I decided to make Hai a list of his new words so he could practice. Miss Hepburn said it was a good idea. She found an empty notebook and paper for us. I started labeling the pages *A, B, C,* and so on through the alphabet. Then I began writing Hai's English words in the notebook under the correct letter.

On page *D* I wrote *Dad.* Hai got the idea. He put *Ba* after my word. On page *G* I wrote *good.* Hai translated, *tôt.* I remembered good sounded like *doe* or *toe,* but I never expected it to be spelled so strangely. I liked the funny-looking mark over the *o.*

Hai flipped to the *M* page. He wrote *Mother,* then *Ma* beside it. Hey, that looked like English. Hai pronounced it *"may."* On the *O* page Hai wrote *OK. OK.* We laughed. I knew he was telling me it was the same in both languages.

Hai kept adding words he knew to his notebook. Then an idea hit me. I could teach him more words. I pointed to the desk. "Desk," I whispered.

"Desk," Hai repeated. We wrote it in Hai's notebook.

"Pen," I said, holding up the pen. Hai echoed it back, and again we added a new word to his notebook.

The two of us cleaned out both desks naming everything: paper, books, pencils, crayons, football cards, scissors, marbles, erasers, jawbreakers. We slipped the jawbreakers quietly in our mouths.

I started labeling my body: hand, finger, fingernail, eye, nose, mouth, teeth. When we reached the belly button, we started giggling.

After school, Hai and I continued labeling everything in sight: grass, sidewalk, steps, school, stoplight, house, car, safety patrol. Hai was busy writing down everything he could point to. Being a tutor was neat.

Hai was going so fast, I was afraid he would get confused and mix everything up. I certainly couldn't remember that many Vietnamese words. To review, I pointed to my eyes and asked Hai to name the word.

"Eye," said Hai.

"Good." I was amazed he had remembered.

We did the same with the elbow and fingers. Hai was unbelievable. I pointed to the sidewalk.

Hai paused a second. He cautiously started, "Side, *uh,* side run."

That was funny, but I didn't want to hurt Hai's feelings. I smiled and said, "Almost, sidewalk."

In one week, Hai and I had pretty well named the objects in the classroom, the things on the way to school, and the parts of our bodies. I decided it was time to take inventory of my house. We labeled the living room and kitchen: couch, lamp, TV, phone, sink, oven, refrigerator, ceiling, rug, cupboard, glass, door, newspaper.

I pulled open a kitchen drawer and started labeling more things: paper clips, rubber bands, cough drops. I had to show Hai what some of the things did, like the bottle opener and the nut chopper. When we got to the tape, Hai's face lit up.

"Tape. Tape." Hai started waving his hands in the

air. I couldn't figure out what he was trying to explain. Hai tore out a page from the back of his notebook. In large letters he printed a sign: chair—cái ghê. He taped the sign to the chair. "Tape. Tape." Now I knew what Hai was saying.

"Yeah, good idea. We'll tape up signs on everything."

I rummaged through my room looking for some paper and marking pens. Hai and I ran to his house and started making signs. I couldn't print them fast enough. Before long, the whole family was in their living room pointing to object after object, demanding its name. In about an hour, the house looked like it had been redecorated in English-Vietnamese wallpaper: table—cai bān, TV—TV, ceiling—trân nhā, floor—nhên nhā, window—caí cua sô, chair cái ghê.

Hai taped a sign "belly button" on his stomach. We laughed.

Thursday at school I told Miss Hepburn about the signs in Hai's home to help the Lings learn English. She suggested we do the same thing to our classroom. The kids loved it. We labeled everything imaginable. In fifteen minutes the room was peppered with words. Spinner and I snuck out into the hall and labeled the drinking fountain.

When I returned, I noticed a note taped to Hai's desk: I SIT NEXT TO AN IDIOT. Hai looked up at me and grinned. Marcie snickered from across the room. I sneered back at her.

By Friday noon, Hai had almost four hundred words in his notebook. He was so proud. He carried the notebook with him wherever he went, as if it were a sack of gold. Kids at lunchtime or recess would name objects for him, and he'd write them down. The kids even began to pantomime actions like jumping rope, coughing, tripping, and hopping. Almost everyone was getting into the act. It was becoming a challenge to find something Hai didn't already have in his book.

Friday after school, Hai and I walked home together. Hai was clutching his most precious possession. We stopped at my house for a snack.

"Hi, boys," Mom greeted us.

"Howdy, Mom. What's there to eat?"

"Fruit. We have apples, oranges, or bananas."

"Yuck! Fruit again?"

"That's it until dinnertime," Mom stated emphatically.

"Aw, Mom," I complained.

Mom looked at me with that do-you-want-me-to-get-mad-at-you-in-front-of-company look?

I grabbed the bananas.

"Well, how many English words has Hai learned today?" Mom asked.

"I was just about to check. I think he's somewhere around four hundred."

Hai straightened up, "No. I know 416!"

Mom laughed. Hai wanted credit for every one of those words.

Hai and I walked into the living room. He wanted to show me his latest accomplishments. Someone had written some new words for Hai. He was bursting with excitement. Proudly, he opened his notebook.

The words nearly jumped off the page. Oh, no.

Hai was learning English all right. The wrong kind of English. I flipped through the pages. Those four-letter words practically leaped out at me. Hai grinned. He had no idea what those words meant. Someone had really played him for a fool. But who? And most of all, why?

7
Partners in Crime

On Saturday Mr. Spinnelli put up the old family tent for Spinner and the gang. The tent smelled pretty gross at first, but we didn't care. We dragged some old blankets and pillows into it. There was just enough room for the Fearsome Foursome.

"What do you guys want to do?" Spinner asked.

I was thinking of what Dad had said, "Try to include Hai in your activities. A.J. will come around." Well, it couldn't hurt to give it a go. A.J. might find out Hai was an OK kid. Was A.J. the culprit who was playing dirty tricks on Hai? Naw. A.J. could be a real creep at times, but he wasn't rotten through and through.

"Be back in a minute, guys," I announced. I dashed out of the tent before anyone could ask where I was going. I ran next door and grabbed Hai.

"Come on, Hai. Spinner's got a tent up." I tried to explain. My pantomime was sketchy at best.

"Tent, *ah*, see."

So Hai and I returned to Spinner's backyard. The guys were busy planning a secret club.

"Partners," suggested Spinner.

"That's an OK name for starters," Pete agreed, "but we need something with more pizzazz."

"Something that sounds dangerous—adventurous—maybe even illegal." A.J. was thinking out loud.

"How about Partners in Crime?" I asked. "We could use just the initials so no one else knows what it stands for."

"*Hum,* Partners in Crime. P in C." We were trying it out for size.

"That's pretty good," Pete announced. So P in C it was. It sounded tough, just what we needed.

"Let's sign a pact in blood," ordered A.J.

"Yeah!" Our voices rang out enthusiastically. I wasn't too crazy about signing anything with my blood, but I was certainly willing to use theirs.

"What's gonna be in this blood-signed pact?" Pete asked cautiously. He must have known I was planning on using his blood.

A.J. started to explain, "Well, for starters we could have a secret sign."

This sounded interesting, and it was delaying the

bloodletting, which was also a good idea. We started racking our brains for secret signals and signs when who should appear at the tent door but pesky Frankie Spinnelli. It never failed: Frankie always appeared just when we were in the middle of cooking up something exciting.

Spinner tried the nice-guy approach, "Why don't you go watch cartoons, Frank-o?"

It didn't work. Frankie knew something was up.

"No!" Frankie pouted. "I want in."

"Frankie, go watch TV." Spinner was starting to blow his cool.

"No. I want in." Frankie was blowing just as hard as Spinner.

Spinner was desperate. He used the tough-guy approach. "Get lost, Freak-o, or I'll turn you into applesauce!"

This got the expected results, "*WHAAAAAAAH! I WANT IN! WHAAAAAAAAH! I WANT IN!*" Frankie was pouring it on so the whole neighborhood could hear.

"This is my tent, and you know it. Bug off!" Spinner grabbed the tent flap and zipped it shut.

Frankie turned his sirens on even louder than before. "*WHAAAAAAAAH! WHAAAAAAAAAH! WHAAAAAH!*" He sounded like he was strung up by his toenails, which wasn't such a bad idea. Mrs. Spinnelli was probably inside now calling the police.

"No," Hai said, pointing to his ear. He meant don't listen, I guess. Hai must know what he's doing. He has two younger sisters and a little brother to put up with.

"WHAAAAAH! WHAAAAH!" Frankie didn't seem to be tiring.

Back to thinking of a secret sign for our club. "How about a skull and crossbones, like pirates?" Pete suggested.

"And we could cross our arms in front of our faces to give the secret sign. Only us guys would know what it means," Spinner continued.

A.J. held up his arms in front of his face announcing, "P in C Forever."

That was neat. We all joined in, "P in C Forever." We chanted with our arms crossed in the air.

"Whaaah. Whaaaah." At last Frankie was wearing down. He began to stop about every thirty seconds to check for results. Each time he'd start up again with a little less enthusiasm.

"Shh," whispered Spinner, "don't make a sound. Maybe he'll think we're gone."

We crouched down low in silence. Frankie stopped. We could tell he was listening.

Softly, Frankie called. "Piiinner? . . . Pinner? . . . Pinner?"

We lay there giggling inside ourselves and noiselessly flashing the P in C Forever sign. Frankie walked around the tent in one direction. He walked around the tent in the other direction. He couldn't figure out where we were. Confused, he tromped back into the house.

"Hurrah!" we roared. "P in C Forever!"

It was about time we put one over on Frankie Spinnelli. It felt great, too, that A.J. and Hai were smiling at the same time. My plan was working, A.J.

just needed to get to know Hai.

"Let's get back to that blood-signed pact." A.J.'s eyes glinted.

I didn't even like it when a mosquito helped itself to my blood.

Spinner saved the moment. "Hey, guys, let's chow down first. I'm starved."

We split to raid refrigerators. I grabbed the Kool-Aid in an old plastic jug without a cover. The only other thing in the fridge was leftover meatloaf. I couldn't take that. It was bad enough the first time. I crawled up to reach the cupboard above the fridge. That's where Mom hides sweets if she has any. What luck. Oreo cookies. I snatched the whole package and raced back to Spinner's.

A.J. arrived with potato chips. Hai brought apples. Pete rounded up grapes and Twinkies. Spinner ran out of the house carrying paper cups and peanut-butter-and-jelly sandwiches. The four of us in the tent shouted, "What's the password?"

"P in C Forever," answered Spinner, crossing his arms unsteadily with the sandwiches and cups in his hands. We let him in.

The five of us stuffed our faces on the loot. The Twinkies went first. We decided to save the leftover Oreos, potato chips, and apples for later. I don't think anyone really wanted an apple, but Hai wasn't too experienced with good old American junk food yet.

Then A.J. announced, "OK, guys, time to bleed. Roll up your sleeve, Hai. Let's see what color your blood is." A.J. started to corner Hai.

What's A.J. after? He was smart enough to know blood was blood. Skin color didn't make any difference.

"Hey, you do it first, A.J." I dared him. "How's Hai supposed to know what this is all about?" Was A.J. bluffing?

"Wait a minute," Pete interrupted. "Let's do that when it's dark. We can do it tonight by candlelight."

Whew! Narrow escape. My heart could start beating again.

"Let's play a game or something," I suggested.

"How about Monopoly?" A.J. asked with a gleam in his eye.

"Yeah," everyone else responded.

"Who's got a game?"

"I do," Pete announced, "but my money isn't all there."

Pete and A.J. took off to Pete's house for the game. Meanwhile, Spinner, Hai, and I ransacked Spinner's house. We crawled under Mr. and Mrs. Spinnelli's bed, tromped over Spinner's soccer shoes in his closet, and rummaged around in Frankie's over-stuffed toy chest. We managed to find only $2,856 in Monopoly money. It was a little mutilated with chocolate fingerprints, but it was better than none.

The three of us headed back for the tent, hoping Pete and A.J. had better luck. Oh, oh. Frankie and Jao were messing around in the tent.

"Scram!" yelled Spinner.

Frankie stuck out a white fungus-coated tongue at us. The three of us stomped toward Frankie and Jao, raising our hands like claws and growling.

That did it. Frankie and Jao streaked out of the backyard scared skinny.

We ducked into the tent. In a minute, Pete and A.J. arrived. "Password?" I asked.

"P in C Forever," they said, flashing the sign.

I opened the flap fast to let them in. Frankie and Jao were hanging around outside again. Quickly they headed for the sandbox when I glared at them.

"Did you find a game?" Spinner asked.

"Sort of. Two cards are missing and my dog chewed some of the rest."

"Well, that's better than we did. Frankie made chocolate chip cookies with most of this money," I added.

"Let's get started. I'll pass out the money. I'm banker," ordered A.J.

Hai didn't have the slightest idea what Monopoly was about, but I could tell he was counting the money in his head.

After three times around the board, no one had enough property to make a monopoly. But I was mighty close. I owned two green deeds. I just needed to maneuver Pete out of North Carolina Avenue, and I'd be rolling in dough.

"Hey, Hai," A.J. poked him. "Trade?" He pointed to the deed he was holding. It was a railroad. A.J. wanted Hai's New York Avenue deed. "See? Trade?" He held up two fingers. "Both $200? Good?"

"Come on, A.J., don't take advantage of Hai," I ordered. "You know New York will give you a monopoly, and Hai will have nothing."

"Aw, cork it, Carlton. Stay out of this." A.J.

sneered, "You gonna baby him all his life? Aren't you tired of being his nursemaid? Let him grow up, creep-o."

I wasn't babying Hai. I wasn't a nursemaid. Someone had to help him. It just didn't seem fair to take advantage of him.

"Shh. Listen," Pete interrupted.

"What?" we whispered.

"I heard something."

We sat motionless. We weren't even breathing.

"I don't hear anything," A.J. spoke out. "Come on, let's get back to the game."

Spinner peered out the front flap. Nothing. "Frankie and Jao aren't in the sandbox anymore. You probably just heard them heading over to Jao's yard."

"Yeah, I guess so," Pete said, though still unconvinced.

"Trade?" A.J. was closing in this time. Hai nodded. A.J. grabbed the deed and made the trade. In a flash, he bought hotels.

"Pete," I tried, "trade me your North Carolina for Illinois Avenue?"

"Naw, you'll have monopoly." Pete studied his deeds. "You got Marvin Gardens?"

"I've got Marvin Gardens," Spinner announced.

So Spinner traded me Illinois for Marvin Gardens, and I traded Marvin Gardens for North Carolina. Now we all had monopolies except Hai. I landed on Virginia and bought it.

"OK, Hai, trade me Virginia for Boardwalk," I motioned.

"Thought that was unfair, Satch," A.J. jeered.

"I'm not taking advantage of him. I'm helping him get a monopoly."

"Looks to me like you're helping yourself right to his best property." A.J. wasn't about to let me explain.

"Look, I couldn't take a railroad because he has a set now. Boardwalk isn't worth anything without Park Place. So what's the big deal?" My face was burning.

"Well, if it's so worthless, then why do you want it at all?"

I stuffed an Oreo into my mouth. I couldn't out-argue A.J. He twisted everything. He didn't want to be fair. He just wanted to be a jerk. And he was doing a good job of it.

I crammed another cookie into my mouth. It tasted crummy. Must be this battle was taking the bite out of my appetite.

The game started up again. Everyone kept landing on A.J.'s property. I was soon going to go bankrupt if someone didn't land on mine.

A.J. was heading toward my green stretch. I'd snag him this time for sure and clean out his bankroll.

"*Shush.* Someone's out there. I know it this time." Pete stiffened.

We listened again. Nothing.

Spinner peaked out the door. Nothing.

Pete was still imagining things.

A.J. rattled the dice. I could feel it. He wouldn't get away this time.

"Hey, what's with these cookies?" Spinner interrupted. "The middle's gone!"

"Let me see 'em." I yanked the package closer for a better look. "Someone's licked out all the frosting and stuck the sides back together. Yuck!"

We all looked at each other. "Frankie and Jao!" we screamed in unison.

Those little culprits. That's what they were doing in the tent while we searched for the Monopoly game. My stomach was turning inside out. I'd eaten at least half a dozen of those germ-infested cookies that Frankie and Jao had slobbered all over. Those mangy monsters. They'd probably infected me with some incurable disease.

I was going to turn them upside down and shake loose what few brains they had. Suddenly—*CRASH!* The tent fell down on us. It felt like a Redi-Mix truck had dumped cement all over me, burying me alive. Everything was black, totally black. I couldn't breathe. I couldn't lift the heavy canvas. Even "help" was muffled in the smothering heap of bodies and tent.

At last I heard Spinner's voice, "I know this has to be Frankie's doing, and when I get my hands on him I'm gonna shred him into coleslaw. . . ."

Hai was talking a mile a minute, too, in Vietnamese. I had the idea he was planning a similar welcome for Jao.

I crawled around on my stomach searching for light and air. Oh, no. My elbow knocked over the Kool-Aid. Now I was covered with sticky purple goo.

Sunlight ahead. Finally, air. My eyes were blurry, trying to adjust to the change in light. Then I saw four spindly little legs ahead—Frankie and Jao. Those sneak thieves. Their top halves came into focus as I approached the tent opening. Their hands were loaded with tent stakes. I was ready to crawl out and clunk their heads together, but my hands and legs were stuck to the tent with purple paste.

The Disasterous Duo had whammied us again. First, the cookie cleanout, and now the tent upheaval. It suddenly dawned on me who were the *real* Partners in Crime.

8
Fire Drill
Freak-out

I spent about two hours in the bathtub after the tenting expedition. By Monday morning, I was back to my normal color—no more purple. Mom has a hairy if I leave for school with so much as a dirty fingernail.

Today in social studies we were naming the states. Maybe that Monopoly game helped Hai with some of the words. What else did he learn from that game? Maybe it wasn't English. Could he see that A.J. was against him? Hai couldn't understand the words, but could he *feel* what A.J. was saying?

HO—ONK! HO—ONK!

The fire drill alarm startled the entire class. Fire drills were neat. It meant at least five minutes less of class time. If we were lucky, sometimes we could squeeze it into ten minutes. There was only one problem with fire drills, we couldn't get caught talking. The Turtle absolutely went berserk if he thought kids were having a good time.

"This is a serious affair," he'd announce over the PA system after every fire drill. "We drill to protect the lives of everyone here should such an emergency arise. . . ." Then The Turtle would remind the student body of the actual burning of Roosevelt School years ago on April Fool's Day. Two people were killed. "It was no joke then, and it's no joke now." The speech never changed. It just seemed longer and more boring with age.

HO—ONK! HO—ONK!

As the alarm kept blasting, the kids lined up at the doorway to file out of the classroom. Then I turned back, remembering Hai. Where was he? He'd never been told what to do in a fire drill. I was sure he hadn't slipped into line ahead of me.

Oh, no. There he was, crouched in a ball underneath his desk. His arms and legs quivered with every pulse of the alarm. Sweat was trickling down his face. His eyes were so wide open his eyeballs were in danger of popping out.

HO—ONK! HO—ONK!

"OK. It's OK, Hai. Come with me," I whispered. I motioned with my hand.

Hai started to breathe a little deeper, but he wouldn't unwrap his arms from around his legs. I bent down and put my hand on his back, trying to calm his quivering body.

"It's OK, Hai. It's just a fire drill. Don't worry." I tried to sound calm, but I could have kicked myself for saying "fire drill." Hai knew the word fire. If that was all he understood, he'd certainly be frightened. What if he thought this was a real fire? I kept rubbing his back and coaxing him to come out from underneath the desk.

HO—ONK! HO—ONK!

Why did that alarm have to be so monstrous sounding? It was enough to blast the bats out of the gym rafters.

At last, Hai half willingly unwrapped his arms from his legs. He crept out from under the desk. I grabbed his hand and lightly tugged him like a dog on a leash. Hai and I caught up with the rest of our class when we reached the outside door. Hai's eyes searched overhead like a radar scanner. With his neck still arched upward, I led Hai to where our class was standing on the playground.

HO—ONK! HO—ONK!

The alarm was fading some as we moved farther away from the building.

A.J. was trying to trip a girl. Pete was stepping on the heels of the kid in front of him. Spinner kept reaching around two people ahead of him to pull Motormouth Marcie's hair.

"Knock it off, you pest. Stop it right now."

Spinner was warming up Marcie's motor fast. Spinner just stared up at the sky trying to pull off the innocent act. That made Marcie's motor burn.

"You're not fooling me, Tony Spinnelli. I'll get even with you for this. I know a few dirty tricks myself," she hissed into Spinner's face.

Marcie was right. She could pull off some mighty rotten tricks. I ought to know. Usually I was her victim. Spinner had better watch out. Marcie could be deadly.

Hai was still shaking some. His eyeballs rolled back and forth surveying the sky. His hand was so sweaty I could hardly hold onto it. I didn't dare let go, though.

Pretty soon A.J. stretched out his arms, turned his voice into an engine, and pretended to be an enemy plane dropping bombs. He soared over three girls and head for Motormouth Marcie. *"Rrrrrrr pakew! Rrrrrrr pakew!"*

A.J. dropped a couple bombs and motioned Pete to join the charade. By this time, the girls were all giggling and ducking A.J.'s arms. They shrieked, but they loved it.

Pete took up where A.J. left off, pretending to man a machine gun on the ground. "Oh, save the women and children first. *Ta-ta-ta-ta-ta*. Pete the Powerful to the rescue."

A.J. and Pete could certainly liven up the place, that was for sure. The kids were laughing, trying not to make too much commotion. Miss Hepburn was halfway across the playground giving the head count from the fire drill to Mr. Tuttle.

Then A.J. headed his bomber straight for Hai and me. With his wings spread out at least six feet wide, he tucked his head down and peered out at us from underneath his eyebrows. *"Rrrrrrr pakew!"* A.J. bombed us. We ducked just in time. He swerved the plane to the left over our heads.

A.J.'s antics started Hai shaking uncontrollably. His body was going up and down like a jackhammer pounding into two tons of cement. This was no time for a war game. Hai was totally confused. First the shrieking of the fire alarm, and now some idiot dive-bombing him with sound effects.

"Hey, A.J., you'd better knock it off around Hai. He doesn't understand you're just playing. The fire drill really shook—"

A.J. heard me, but he reeled around and came at Hai for a second attempt.

"RRRRRRRRRR PAKEW!" A.J. dove at Hai again.

"Knock it off, A.J.!" I screamed. Every muscle in Hai's sweaty body trembled with terror. He could hardly stand up after that last dive from A.J.

A.J. wasn't about to lie low. "What's the matter? You two afraid of a little noise? What do you do when it thunders? Poor baby. Do you suck your thumb, too?"

A.J. was going too far. I didn't know how much of this Hai understood, but I hoped it was nothing. Hai didn't deserve to be made fun of. He probably was really bombed in Vietnam. He probably had to run for his life when the alarms sounded. A.J. wasn't dumb. He could figure it out. A.J. knew Hai's country had been at war for years. This was no game to Hai. Why couldn't A.J. just leave Hai alone?

A.J. lowered his head again and stretched out his

arms. He stood staring at the two of us as if he were in a trance.

My hands were sweating as I flexed my fingers. Blood was rushing to my face. I gritted my teeth. My jaw clamped closed so tightly all the things I wanted to say couldn't come out.

A.J. turned on his motor and steadily and deliberately headed toward Hai and me. He looked as if he really wanted to kill us. His upper lip was raised to attack. *"RRRRRRRRRRR,"* A.J. stalked us like a fox ready to leap at its prey. Hai's trembling body was about to remove my arm from its socket.

Just as A.J. was within inches of letting loose a bomb over our head, my hand leaped out from my body and smacked into A.J.'s unprotected gut. I didn't realize what I'd done until I saw A.J. doubled over in agony.

Slowly, A. J. straightened up. Now his eyes filled with fire. A.J. reeled his right arm up and landed his fist square on the left half of my face. I felt like my head had just been smashed in a trash compactor. Everything sort of whirled around. A few seconds later I realized I was on the ground looking up at two hundred heads hovering over me.

With that kind of crowd, The Turtle soon appeared. He peeled away the bodies encircling me until he reached the center.

"What's this all about? Who's involved here? This is no way to conduct a fire drill. . . ."

My head was still vibrating. I couldn't even sit up yet. I was in no condition to listen to one of his famous fire drill speeches.

"You pick yourself up. The two of you march straight to my office. This is a terrible example to set in front of the younger grades. Sixth graders. You ought to be ashamed of yourselves. . . ." The Turtle continued mumbling to himself as everyone else was motioned back to their classrooms.

A.J. and I stumbled into The Turtle's office. I knew we'd be given the third degree. What could I say? A.J. was definitely being a first-class jerk. He deserved to be socked. I didn't. If I ratted on him to the principal, though, the gang would never forgive me. Why do I always lose?

Mr. Tuttle sat us down and closed the door. The place looked like a prison cell. The Turtle sat behind his ten-foot desk like a judge and jury rolled into one. He peered down at us as if we were murderers. Hey, all I did was give A.J. exactly what he deserved.

"All right, Sidney, you start. What happened?" The Turtle demanded.

"Well, *uh*," I tried to stall, "I *uh*, hit A.J. because, *uh*, because I thought he tripped me. Things got a little out of control after that."

"Out of control? I should say!" The Turtle snapped at A.J. next. "And what's your story, Alex?"

"*Um, uh,* my foot was sort of in his way, and I guess he thought I did it on purpose. After he hit me, I punched him. That's all."

"Well, you two are wrong about one thing. That isn't all. You will report to me after school for one hour of cleanup duty each. Next time, I won't be so kind." The Turtle glared at us as his neck jutted forward out of his shell. "Do you understand me?"

"Yes, sir."

"Yes, sir."

I hung my head and tried to look remorseful. Actually I still wanted to pulverize A.J. My eye was puffing. I probably looked like a cyclops, with one oversized eye bulging out of my head. And my nose had now relocated beneath my right earlobe. My whole head throbbed. The Turtle made us shake hands. Dumb. I still hated A.J. for the way he acted.

"You're dismissed. I'll see you both at 3:15 sharp," Mr. Tuttle ordered. "Oh, and, Sidney, you'd better get an ice pack from the first-aid station. Your eye doesn't look too good. You're going to have quite a shiner by the looks."

Why did he have to say that? That was as good as telling A.J. he had trounced me. I wished A.J. would throw up right on The Turtle's desk. At least I'd know A.J.'s gut was hurting as much as my eye.

After school I pushed the broom around the hallway. A.J. emptied wastebaskets. Neither one of us spoke when we passed by each other. I thought about tripping A.J. with my broom. No, I'd just end up the villain again. I couldn't win.

As the dust flew in front of me, this rotten day turned over and over in my mind. Fear of the alarm had made Hai freak out. Who wouldn't act a little crazy if he'd seen buildings collapse and dead bodies all over during a bombing raid? Hai was certainly entitled to be afraid when that strange siren went off.

But A.J.? What was his problem? Why did A.J. freak out? Dad's words kept wandering around in my head, "Maybe this tough-guy approach of A.J.'s is really a cover-up." What could A.J. be covering up? "Maybe A.J. is actually a little afraid of Hai." With a punch like the one I was wearing, it was hard to imagine A.J. could be afraid of anything.

9
A Sticky Situation

As days passed, the silence between A.J. and me seemed deadly. Would things get better when soccer season started? Coach Spinnelli got Hai assigned to our soccer team, the Space Speeders.

Last year, with the Fearsome Foursome in command, our team won four out of six games. We came in third place in the league. Now I wasn't even so sure about third place. Without the Fearsome Foursome pulling together, we couldn't possibly win.

The first practice of the season was Wednesday after school. "OK, line up over there," ordered Mr. Spinnelli. "We'll start warming up by dribbling the ball downfield in pairs. After everyone's had a chance to pass and dribble, we'll scrimmage."

Coach Spinnelli was sending pairs downfield. "Dribble tight. Dribble tight," he yelled after Spinner and Pete.

"OK, you two, you're up next," Coach ordered, pointing to Hai and me. "Let's see what you can do."

I knew Coach wanted to size up Hai. I didn't want Hai to be embarrassed if he flubbed it. I was sure Hai would catch on once he understood the game. I patted Hai on the back to reassure him.

I started dribbling downfield. Hai stayed across from me. So far, he had the idea. I passed the ball to Hai. "Come on, Hai. Corner the ball and dribble it in close."

Hai charged the ball confidently. Oh, no, he was going to kick it too hard and lose control. But could I warn him? The ball came right to him. Hai cornered the ball and started dribbling downfield. The ball was sticking to his foot like glue, and he was charging full speed ahead. Hai was a pro! I stood there with lead in my shoes. And I was worried about Hai looking foolish. I was the nitwit.

Hai flicked the ball into the air by curling up his toe. He whizzed a pass over to me using his right hip. Neato. Perfect aim. Before we were through, Hai had passed the ball to me with everything from the hair on his head to the toenails on his left foot. One thing was for sure: I wasn't going to be explaining soccer to Hai, he would be explaining it to me.

When Saturday morning arrived, we gathered for our first game against the Kickers. Friday night's rain had left the field mushy, but Spinner hadn't lost his touch. He could still weave through the fullbacks, fake to the left, and zip the ball into the right side of the goal before anyone realized what happened. He scored two points in the first three minutes of the game. Then the Kickers' coach told a couple gorillas to stick to Spinner. He was wrapped up like a mummy in a mass of opposing players.

Meanwhile on the sidelines, Frankie had ants in his pants. He just couldn't stay off the playing field. Mrs. Spinnelli and my mom kept passing him back and forth. For a while, Frankie occupied himself by going through Mrs. Spinnelli's purse. He even tried to put on her lipstick. The guys on the bench were doubling over with laughter. Frankie's charades were taking their toll on our concentration. The other team managed to tie up the score 2-2.

At halftime Coach Spinnelli assigned us new positions. He wanted to get some other guys in scoring position—me and Hai. I hoped we could come through.

The ball was in play. The Kickers tried to score. A.J., our goalie, caught the ball and threw it out to Pete. Pete dribbled downfield and passed to me. I tried to sidekick it in the left corner of the goal but missed. Quickly, Hai recovered it. He tried a Spinner fake-left-score-right combination. *Yeah.* It worked. The score was now 3-2. The Space Speeders were speeding away at last.

Even A.J. was jumping up and down with excitement. *Hmm.* Maybe soccer would be the glue to stick our friendship back together.

But Frankie was back to making a nuisance of himself by running onto the playing field. Our team was in danger of a penalty. That could cost us the one-point lead. No one seemed to be able to tame that monkey.

Coach pulled me off the field for a substitute. "Come here, Frank-o," I coaxed. Frankie didn't fall for it. He knew I wanted to corral him between Pete and me. Then I remembered how much Frankie loved to sit on his dad's shoulders. "Come on, Frankie. Come on and sit on Old Satch's shoulders. You'll be way up high like the big boys." Frankie reluctantly approached me.

I bent down, put my head between Frankie's legs, and scooped him up onto my shoulders. He was really happy and safe up there. Frankie kept chattering to himself, "ooooh . . . ball . . . kick." Once in a while, Frankie pulled on my hair or put his hands over my eyes, but that was okay. I had solved the problem of keeping Frankie off the playing field.

The Space Speeders were still in the lead. If we could just hold onto it for two more minutes, we'd have our first victory. Frankie entertained himself up on my shoulders. "Run . . . ooooh . . . wet . . . sticky." I didn't care what Frankie talked about, just so he stayed put until the game was over. He kept tugging at my hair every now and then, so I bounced him up and down a little to keep him busy.

One minute left. The Kickers had the ball now. "Come on, Speeders, get that ball back." They shot—and missed. A.J. grabbed the ball and fed it to Pete. *Yea!* We were out of that sticky situation now.

Ouch. Frankie was tugging at my hair, but I could stand it for one more minute if that's what it took to win the game.

Thirty seconds. "Come on, team. You can do it." *Ouch!* That last tug on my hair was really something.

Ten seconds. Nine. Eight. Seven. Six. This was it. I reached up for Frankie. It was almost time to run out onto the field and join in the celebration. Three. Two. Yuck! What was so sticky? What was in my hair? It was all over me. Gum. "Frankie Spinnelli, you animal!" He had stretched green Hubba Bubba from one ear to the other. My hair was wrapped in a web a million spiders couldn't make.

Mrs. Spinnelli gasped and took Frankie off me. He started screaming and crying, "Satch took my gum. Mommy, Mommy make him give it back. Satch steal my gum." He wailed on and on, as if I wanted that gum stuck in my hair.

Mom just shook her head. Then she broke out laughing. Even Hai and A.J. were laughing. They all started pointing.

"Satch," Mom laughed, "your hair, it's . . ." She could hardly spit out the words. This didn't seem funny at all to me. "Your hair is covered with lipstick, too. You're really a sight."

Oh, creeping crud. Why me? Why does Frankie Spinnelli always zap me?

When we got home, Mom took some ice and scissors to cut out the chewed-up mess entangled in my hair. The little hair left she scrubbed with Lava soap. What a price to pay for victory, only eleven and already bald.

10
Someone to
Count On

For four Saturdays in a row the Space Speeders were victorious. My hair was beginning to grow back, Frankie Spinnelli was permanently banished from the field, and Hai was scoring two, sometimes three, points a game. Even A.J. had cooled it. Maybe he realized Hai wasn't a wimp. Maybe he saw that Hai was fitting in after all.

This Saturday we were playing the Way Out Whiz Kids. They were undefeated, too. Undoubtedly, the winner of this game would be league champs. The Whiz Kids were even faster than their name. Last year we huffed and puffed after them the entire game.

They trounced us five to one. This year with our secret weapon, Hai, we stood an even chance of beating them.

Game time. Ball control was grabbed by the Whiz Kids at center field. Hai immediately charged, kicking the ball between the other player's feet. The guy was so startled, he stopped dead in his tracks. Two Whiz Kids started to close in on Hai. Hai darted between them as if he were jumping into an elevator just as the doors were shutting. Hai passed the ball to me. I dribbled about ten feet when three Whiz Kids rushed toward me. I passed the ball to Spinner who was in scoring position. If he could just find a hole to shoot through, Spinner could rack up the first point. Spinner tried his dependable fake-left-score-right combination. Blocked. The Whiz Kids were too smart for his maneuver.

Just then I noticed Hai in a scramble by the goal. Spinner's kick had been blocked all right, but Hai was on the alert. Just as the ball flew into the air, Hai shot about three feet off the ground, bunted the ball with his head, and landed a goal directly in their net. *Yea!* Space Speeders in the lead:1-0.

Ball control changed back and forth lots of times. Finally, I stole the ball and headed downfield. Suddenly, it seemed like half a dozen Whiz Kids had surrounded me. With a hard kick, I passed the ball over their heads to Hai. Crummy pass. The ball was way out of Hai's reach. Hai leaped sideways into the air. He seemed suspended in midflight as he stretched out his body to kick the ball. It streaked through the air into the left corner of the goal. What a play! This could only happen with pros! 2-0. Whiz Kids were fast becoming the Was Kids.

As the third quarter started, the Whiz Kids made their move. The heat was on. A.J. tried to protect our goal. He saved about a dozen clear shots. We were lucky the Whiz Kids only tied it up 2-2.

Just before the fourth quarter started, A.J. came off the field looking worried. "Come on, you guys. Get in there and hussle. I can't protect that goal all by myself."

Hai, Spinner, and I headed out to do our stuff. Actually, all Spinner and I had to do was feed the ball to Hai, and he'd do the rest.

Spinner took ball control. He shot directly to me. I dribbled down toward scoring range. I could hardly find Hai's yellow shirt among the fire-red shirts of the Whiz Kids. Hai tried to dodge in and out. Every time I caught a glimpse of yellow, it quickly became red. I passed the ball to Pete, hoping he could get within range of Hai. Pete passed back to Spinner. We were getting nowhere. Spinner passed the ball back to me. I tried a long shot. It wasn't even close. Hai managed to get one toe on the ball before he was smothered by red T-shirts. The Whiz Kids took command. They made a quick getaway downfield to our goal.

A.J. snapped to attention. "Defense. Defense," he screamed. Our fullbacks, slow to react, gave open territory to the red shirts. A.J. didn't stand a chance defending the goal against the onslaught. *Boom.* Score for the Whiz Kids.

"Where were you guys?" hollered A.J. "How come

they can get downfield in half the time it takes you turkeys to move three steps?"

"No sweat. There's plenty of time. Hai'll score, just as soon as he's in the clear. We can count on Hai," I assured A.J.

"Sure. Sure." A.J. didn't sound too convinced.

I turned to catch up with the action. I could hear A.J. sputtering under his breath, "Count on him, nothing. I wouldn't count on that lousy creep if my life depended on it."

So A.J. was still gunning for Hai. But why? Hai had proven himself. He was one of the team. He was our ticket to the league championship. We'd dreamed of that for two years.

I followed the herd downfield. Two minutes left. We could score, if we got our act together. Pete managed to get the ball to Hai. Great! Hai had clear range of the goal. He drew back his left to slug the ball into the net. The championship would be ours. Hai couldn't possibly miss. Suddenly, Hai fell to the ground, screaming in pain. He grabbed his right leg at the calf and started hitting it. Hai's body doubled up into a little ball.

The whole team raced to Hai, trying to help. "What's the matter?" everyone asked.

Time was called.

Hai was in so much pain he couldn't talk. He gasped for air as he kept socking his leg. His neck muscles bulged as he gritted his teeth in agony.

Coach Spinnelli tore out onto the field. He bent down and peeled Hai's hands away from his leg. Coach started rubbing Hai's calf. Hai was breathing more regularly now. The muscles in Hai's neck weren't sticking out quite so much, but he was still in pain. His eyes were still clamped shut. Coach kept massaging Hai's leg.

Coach seemed to know what he was doing. Hai wasn't screaming out in pain anymore. "I think Hai has a charley horse," Coach Spinnelli explained.

"Charley horse?" asked Hai. He finally was able to open his eyes.

"Yes, charley horse. It's a name for a muscle spasm. Here, feel this hard knotlike thing bulging from your leg." Coach kept rubbing Hai's leg as he took Hai's hand to show him the problem. "Your muscle is out of control. It's like a cramp."

"*Ahhh,*" Hai answered. "Better."

Hai stood up with a limp. It was obvious he was still in pain, but he wasn't about to quit. He wanted to win as much as anyone.

"No, Hai," Coach Spinnelli ordered. "I can't let you take the risk." Coach helped Hai off the playing field. He continued to massage Hai's leg.

"Win. Win. Play. Play," Hai kept saying, though still in agony.

"A win at your expense would never be worth it to me. No, Hai. You rest." Coach was emphatic. "Come on, you guys, pull together. You can still do it. Don't throw in the towel yet."

We tried to gear up our enthusiasm, but enthusiasm wasn't enough. The game ended with the Way Out Whiz Kids victorious: 3-2. The league championship was theirs. It had slipped right through our fingers.

A.J. slithered over to me on the way off the field. "Who's that guy you said we could count on, Satch? Was it some chap by the name of Charlie Horse?" He raised his fingers to his eyes again, ready to perform his Chinaman imitation.

"Bug off, A.J., before I finish what I started at the fire drill." Instantly, I knew that was the wrong subject to bring up.

"You mean one black eye wasn't enough for you?" A.J. jeered.

How could I have forgotten? For three weeks the world had watched the color change on the left half of my face. First, my eye was puffy red. Then it turned a deep purplish black. For days and days it got blacker and blacker. Finally it lightened up to a pukey yellowish green before it faded into stripes. I looked like a yellow, green, and white zebra. I didn't think I'd ever be human again.

"Well, if that's what you want, Satch, old buddy, I'll give you a matched set this time. You can count on me!" A.J. sneered.

All the things I wanted to say to A.J. just rattled around in my brain. I could feel the blood rushing to my head. My hands were sweating. My mouth went dry. If I didn't clear out of there soon, I could count on A.J. to deliver just what he promised. That was for sure!

What a rotten friend I was, too chicken to defend Hai when he really needed me.

11
The Main Event

Ten days before Thanksgiving the soccer award banquet was held at our church, our team's official sponsor. Hai's family sat across from Mom, my sisters, and me. The Lings bobbed and smiled at the people who greeted them. The kids knew a fair amount of English, but the language was still difficult for the parents and grandmother.

The Spinnellis arrived and sat next to Hai's family. The aroma of ham and baked beans filled the air. The jumble of voices hummed loudly as more and more people entered the room.

A.J.'s family was seated at the next table. If I

looked straight between Hai's mom and dad, I could see A.J., but I didn't want to. Ever since we lost the league championship, A.J. and I did not even look at each other, let alone speak. I guess the Fearsome Foursome was nothing but history. Instead of bringing us together, soccer had ended up tearing us apart. It looked like I had chosen between Hai and A.J. after all. A.J. simply could not be reasoned with. He didn't want to work things out, and there was nothing in the world I could do to make him.

Reverend Miller clanked a knife on a glass to get the crowd's attention. "Before we start the meal, let us offer a blessing to the one who makes all this abundance of food possible."

Heads bowed. I wasn't sure what Hai's family would do. Did they believe in God? They didn't go to our church, or to Spinner's church, either. They didn't go to any church that I knew of. Did they know what we were doing? They bowed their heads like everyone else.

Reverend Miller prayed, "Dear Lord, as we gather here to honor our young athletes, we offer thanks for the food we are about to receive. We ask that you not only nourish these young boys in body, but you keep them mindful of the nourishment faith gives. We pray also for our adopted family, the Lings, who you have brought here from Vietnam. Help us truly to make this land a real home for them. Help us understand what the ravages of war do to all peoples, so that we may save future generations from its pain. We ask these things in Jesus' name, our Lord. Amen."

As I straightened up, my eyes drifted over to A.J.'s table. Strangely, his mother was wiping her eyes with a tissue. Mr. Jackson gently patted her back to comfort her. He was kind of sniffling, too. What was that all about? I had to turn away. I couldn't let A.J. see me watching them. Must be the winter cold season, that's all.

Our table was called to the serving area. Tables full of food stretched the entire length of the room. I could hardly wait to dive into the chocolate cake, apple pie, peach cobbler, brownies. . . . My stomach was doing flip-flops just waiting in line. The Lings pointed and chattered in Vietnamese. I bet they'd never seen so much food all at one time.

Suddenly, my mind flashed to the pictures we were shown in *National Geographic*. I remembered Asian kids staring at the cameras. Their bones looked as if they were about to poke through their skin. Their heads looked too large for their frail bodies. And their stomachs had bulged out because of starvation. As bad as their stomachs looked, it was the eyes that got to me. Those sad brown eyes were haunting. They stared into emptiness. Thinking of that made me feel less like pigging out.

When the meal was over, the ceremony began. Of course, we all knew the main event was the awarding of the league championship trophy. The one and only Whiz Kids had wrapped that up.

Smaller trophies were awarded for second and third place. I guess winning second place was no disgrace, but I have to admit first place would have been a lot more fun.

Now the individual awards were being announced. We didn't know these winners yet. The speaker at the microphone said, "It is with a great deal of pleasure that I make this next award to the Coach of the Year. He is a man who is a winner off the field as well as on. He has given his time and energy for the good of his boys, and he's always willing to encourage a new player. . . ."

He *had* to be talking about Coach Spinnelli. I hoped he'd win. He's really the greatest. Coach didn't just use good strategy to clinch a game, he played every player, good or bad. I knew Coach wanted that first-place trophy as much as we did, but he didn't let that get in the way with doing what was right for Hai. Coach could have sent him back into that game after his charley horse, but he wasn't about to take chances with Hai's leg.

The speaker continued, "Without further ado, I would like to introduce the Coach of the Year—the Whiz Kids' coach, Mr. Gary . . . "

Aw, rats. Coach Spinnelli didn't get it. What a downer. Mr. Spinnelli smiled and applauded, too. He didn't seem at all disappointed. Didn't it matter to him?

Referees were given plaques. Honorable mention ribbons were passed out to about thirty guys. I got one. So did Spinnner and A.J.

"And now we come to our last award this evening," the emcee announced. "The League High Scorer's trophy goes to a boy who managed to rack up seventeen goals this season. A few short months ago, he didn't even live in Owosso. In fact a few short months ago, he didn't even live in America. Come on up here, Hai Ling. This trophy is yours. Congratulations."

Cheers erupted. Hai didn't know what all this was. He'd heard his name, but that was about all.

"You won, Hai! You won!" I screamed. "Go get your trophy." I was jumping off my seat. Hai looked baffled.

Coach Spinnelli came over to Hai and walked him up to the podium. Hai half grinned as a man handed him a mounted golden soccer player. *Wow.* It was gorgeous. Coach congratulated Hai with a pat on the back. Still confused, Hai followed Coach back to their seats.

Everyone on the team came over to inspect Hai's trophy. Everyone, that is, except A.J. Hai didn't say much. He just smiled politely.

People collected their picnic baskets and headed for the parking lot. Surprise. Snow was everywhere. And it was still coming down. All the kids opened their mouths and tried to eat the falling flakes. Hai's family stood in disbelief.

"No see before," Hai gasped. He kept turning around and around. He didn't want to miss watching one flake fall.

"Snow," I called.

"Snow, snow, snow, snow. . . ." Hai laughed and danced around. He was like a puppy prancing around on a newly waxed floor. I'd seen Hai happy before, but this was a new kind of happy. He was so free. He almost seemed to float in the air with the flakes of snow.

As I lay in bed watching the giant blobs of white drift downward, I could picture Hai prancing around. Discovering snow was more exciting to him than winning the League High Scorer's trophy. How could a smart kid like Hai completely miss the main event?

12
The Snow
Phantom

Blam! A snowball landed right in the middle of my back.

Whizzz! I returned the throw. Hai ducked. My snowball sailed just two inches over his head. Hai was wasting no time learning about snow.

Another one! This time I jumped to the side and avoided Hai's perfect aim.

A hit! Wow! My snowball landed right on Hai's neck. He looked startled. "Enough?" I shouted, a little sorry that I'd hit him after all.

"Enough. Cold," said Hai, as he cleaned out the snow from under his collar.

Hai and I climbed the steps on Spinner's porch. Spinner was inside, gulping the last of his orange juice.

"Come on, Spinner. Step on it. If we get to school early, we can play King of the Mountain," I called.

Once there, we spotted the right snowbank and climbed up. Beating my chest and giving the Tarzan call, I announced ownership, *"Ah—ah—ah!"* Hai looked at me like I belonged in the nuthouse.

In seconds a crowd of kids rushed at the three of us. Spinner and I held off about eight of them before being overtaken by an army of puny fourth graders. Hai peered out from underneath a pile of bodies that had mashed him into a snow cone. He muttered something in Vietnamese that sounded like, "Why didn't you creeps tell me this was gonna happen?"

Snow not only meant fun. It meant lots of moolah. I could get rich shoveling walks. I hated the work, but the way I figured it, I could earn about half the cost of the dirt bike I wanted. The rest of the money I should be able to get from selling my old bike.

After school, I grabbed my snow shovel to get started making my fortune. Mom called out the door after me, "Satch, why don't you shovel our walk first?"

"Aw, Mom, ours can wait. I'll do it later," I pleaded.

"OK. Don't forget now," Mom warned.

I could always shovel our walk, but my customers might not wait. Besides, my customers paid more than Mom did. Since Dad and Mom were divorced, Mom called shoveling the snow "my responsibility."

What it really meant was I got to break my back for half the price.

First stop, Mrs. Raymond's house. She lived alone and always wanted a "polite young man" to clear her walks after a fresh snow. Besides that, she had an easy sidewalk—smooth and straight. I rounded the corner toward the Raymond house. Last winter the job paid three dollars. Maybe this year she'd pay three fifty or four. The money was almost jingling in my pocket when I suddenly noticed—Mrs. Raymond's walk was already shoveled. What a dirty trick. Some sneak thief stole my job. Well, maybe her grandson or somebody visited her. He probably shoveled the walk as a favor.

Better luck at my next stop, the Bradleys'. The Bradleys usually hired me. They lived on a corner and had twice as much sidewalk as most people. In heavy snow I could pocket five or six dollars easy. The Bradleys' house was just coming into view. Oh, no! The whole walk was completely cleared. Not a flake of snow remained. Who could have shoveled it? Mr. Bradley didn't get home from work until after dark. Mrs. Bradley couldn't shovel anything in her condition. She was expecting a baby soon. Someone was definitely ahead of me. Whoever it was, he was snatching up all my best customers.

I hustled down Clark Avenue toward the Lees' house. Surely the Lees would need their walk shoveled. Whoever was stealing my customers couldn't possibly have had time to clear three walks in the one hour and a half since school let out. Oh, no! Foiled again. The walk was so clean it looked as if cement carpeting had just been laid.

This was too much. Someone had just robbed me of twelve dollars. The dirt bike was going to rot in the store while I stretched my arms down to my ankles from carrying this stupid snow shovel around the world. Who was this snow phantom luring away my loyal customers? How could this muscleman shovel so fast?

Discouraged, I headed home.

Just as I dragged myself up the porch steps, Mom nagged me, "Sidney, when are you going to shovel our walk?"

"Yeah. Yeah. I'll get it done. It's starting to get dark. I'll do it tomorrow."

Wednesday morning before school, King of the Mountain was in full swing. I managed to shove Motormouth Marcie right into another girl. The two of them rolled into A.J. He immediately toppled over and clunked his head on Miss Hepburn's car fender. Marcie ranted and raved, screaming about the dent in the fender.

"We're gonna tell Miss Hepburn exactly how you did that, Sidney Carlton. You won't think you're such hot stuff when she hears what you've done to her car." Marcie huffed away. She wasn't really going to tell Miss Hepburn. She'd get into just as much trouble as me.

The real problem was A.J. He wasn't worried about the dent in the fender either. It was the dent in his head he was thinking about. A.J. started stalking right toward me. He was wearing the face he'd had on when he bombed Hai and me at the fire drill.

Those fiery eyes spelled revenge. If I didn't think of something quick, I was going to end up as a hood ornament on Miss Hepburn's car.

What could I do? I couldn't back down again the way I did at the soccer game. I couldn't let him cream me again with a cyclops eye.

Brrrring! Saved by the bell.

"*Ah—ah-ah!*" I let out my famous Tarzan call. Then before A.J. had a chance to prove I wasn't victorious, I jumped off the snow mountain and ran to line up at the school entrance.

That afternoon we drew names for the class Christmas gift exchange. As usual, I drew a girl. Boys' gifts are easy to think of. They like neat things. But girls' stuff. Yuck! Who wants to walk into a store and buy perfume or bubble bath?

"What do with name?" Hai asked after class.

"You give that person a present at the Christmas party," I tried to explain.

"Cwizmas?" Hai was totally confused even though Miss Hepburn had tried to explain this to him. I guess he'd never celebrated Christmas before.

"Christmas, Hai. It's a holiday. We give people presents—gifts. Christmas is the birthday of Jesus Christ. Christ is the word in Christmas. It's just pronounced a little different."

Hai nodded his head. I knew he really didn't understand it all.

"Let's see whose name you drew." I unfolded Hai's piece of scrap paper. Oh, no. This was worse than a girl. It was A.J. How in the world could Hai ever give A.J. a present?

Friday it snowed again. This time I grabbed my shovel immediately when I arrived home from school. I had to get my old customers back before that snow phantom invaded my territory again.

Mrs. Raymond's house was in sight. Good. Her walk wasn't shoveled. I hopped up her porch steps two at a time. I rang the bell. She appeared at the door, a little surprised to see me.

"Hello, Sidney."

"Hi, Mrs. Raymond. Would you like me to shovel your walk?" I asked extra politely.

"Well, ordinarily that would be just fine, but I've hired a very nice young man to do it all winter. It's a little cheaper for me this way. You know, things get more and more expensive every year, and I live on a fixed income . . . ." Mrs. Raymond went on and on.

"OK, well, see ya." I couldn't think of anything else to say.

"Thank you for thinking of me. Good-bye." Mrs. Raymond closed the door.

What was going on? Who was cheaper? Who got this job all winter? Well, I guess she needed the money.

I hightailed it to the Bradleys. I could see their walk was still covered with snow. *Whoopee!* At least I beat the snow phantom.

Mrs. Bradley came to the door. She was as big as a refrigerator. Surely, she'd want me to clear that huge sidewalk.

"Sorry, Satch. I hired a boy for the season. He's so reasonable, I just couldn't pass it up. With the new baby about to arrive and all, we have to watch every penny." Mrs. Bradley was beginning to sound just like Mrs. Raymond.

Whoever this phantom was, he had a real sales pitch, he was muscle-bound, and he was *cheap*. Who knew the neighborhood so well? Someone was trying to steal money right out of my wallet. A.J.? He still wanted revenge. If he couldn't smash in my face, was he trying to clean out my cash register?

I walked by the Lees' house. The snow was freshly shoveled. Yep! The snow phantom had been here and vanished. The only thing to do was head back home and shovel my own walk for a couple lousy bucks. At least Mom would be off my back for a while about an eleven-year-old's responsibility. And two bucks was better than the big zero I had at the moment.

Just as I rounded the corner toward home, I could see someone shoveling the sidewalk in front of *my* house. It couldn't be my sisters. Carrie and Lisa might have a horrible accident, like breaking a fingernail, if they shoveled the walk.

What if it was Mom? Oh, oh, I was in big trouble. I could feel a big lecture brewing. "This walk has been sitting here for four days waiting for you. I don't expect you to do that much around here. Would you like to wait four days for your next meal? Honestly, Sidney Carlton, some days I don't know if you're growing up or growing down."

Just thinking of the lecture made me feel guilty. I really wasn't facing up to my share of the work around the house. Maybe I wasn't growing up after all.

As I crept closer to home, the figure kept tossing

snow off to the side. Mom was really pouring it on.

As I inched closer, I could see an orange hat. Where had I seen that hat before? Hai! What was Hai doing shoveling my walk?

I ran up and shouted, "Hai, what are you doing?"

Startled at first, Hai straightened up. "Satch, hello. You like? I have four jobs. I do good work?"

"Why are you here?" I demanded.

"I shovel. Your mom say OK. One dollar." Hai grinned proudly.

"One dollar? Are you crazy?"

"I make six dollar every time it snow. I have four jobs all winter. Good? No?" Hai stood there pleased with himself.

Zowie! Hai was the muscle-bound snow phantom. He was the creep robbing me of my dirt bike money. He was the freak undercutting me right under my nose. Worst of all, my own mother had been taken in. I threw my shovel against the house. For one lousy dollar Hai could have this stinkin' job.

13
Fragile—Handle with Care

I couldn't put off shopping any longer. Our class Christmas party would be Friday, the last day of school before vacation.

Thursday after school I stopped downtown at the dime store. I still had to spend my hard-earned money on a Christmas present for a girl. Hair ribbons? Naw, that was too corny for a boy to give to a girl. She might think I liked her. Magic markers? Better, but she probably had some already.

I strolled down the middle aisle. A model? I picked it up. This was a new item on the shelves. Decent. A Corvette Stingray. In silver. Neato. This was definitely not for a girl, but it demanded a second look.

Suddenly, Hai appeared from out of nowhere.

"Shopping?" he asked.

"Yeah." What did it look like? Hai wasn't exactly the person I most wanted to see, especially if he was here spending the money I should have had.

"Present for Cwizmas?"

"Yeah. I have to buy a present for the party."

"This?" asked Hai, pointing to the model in my hands.

"No, this is a present for a boy. I was just looking it over." I set the model back on the shelf.

Hai browsed through the puzzles and magazines. "This OK?" he asked, holding up a comic book.

"Yeah, it's OK." If Hai was buying A.J.'s gift, a crummy comic book was plenty good enough.

My eyes lit on something. Stationery. Girls love to write silly letters. Flowers lined the top and a ladybug sat at the bottom. Perfect. That would do the trick. I grabbed the box and headed for the checkout counter without saying any more to Hai.

Friday afternoon finally arrived. The party got under way when Motormouth Marcie screamed out, "It's here. The food is here!" Marcie would likely have gulped it all down herself if Miss Hepburn hadn't rescued it.

First order of business was the gift exchange. When Hai went over to A.J.'s desk, A.J. looked him in the belt buckle and grunted out a half "thanks."

Hai didn't seem to be bothered. He spoke right up so A.J. would be certain to hear him, "Merry

Cwizmas, I wiss you much happy for Cwizmas." How could Hai be so nice to him after all the rotten things A.J. pulled?

Curiosity was gnawing at my bones. Who drew my name? If it was a girl, I hoped it wouldn't be a creepy gift. Girls love junk that smells terrible.

Oh, no! Motormouth Marcie was making her way down my row. My stomach dropped clear down to the floor. *Please,* I said to myself, *don't let her stop at my desk. Please?* Marcie glared me right in the eye. She kept coming my way. Why me? Why did I always get burned?

Marcie hung over me. She laid a crumpled-up red-and-white box on my desk. It looked as if she'd fished the wrapping paper out of the garbage can.

"Merry Christmas, Satch." Marcie grinned. "Keep the box turned up this way. I don't want you to break anything." Marcie loved to make me look stupid.

"Yeah, OK," I mumbled. That must mean there was glass inside the mangled box. Glass could only mean one thing—stinky stuff for sure.

At last, all the deliveries were completed. Now it was time to see what ghastly aroma awaited me inside that flea-bitten box. The paper was in such bad shape that the top was covered with holes.

I yanked the bow off. The box jiggled. I ripped off the paper. An old shoe box with holes in the top. Dumb Marcie. Really dumb. Couldn't you even find a decent box? I peeled off the tape holding the lid down when—

"*EEEEEEK!*" I screamed and fell off my chair. Something jumped out of the box and into my face.

Recovering my balance, I saw a piece of brown fur scoot down the aisle toward Miss Hepburn's desk.

"Oh, it's a mouse!" a girl screamed as she hopped up on a table. It wasn't long before half the class was shrieking in unison, and the other half was perching atop desks.

Spinner crawled under Miss Hepburn's desk trying to corner the creature. It wriggled out of his hand into the hallway. Gone forever.

Even in a crisis, Marcie's motor wouldn't run down. "It isn't a mouse," she sobbed. "It's a baby gerbil. It's a very original gift, and if that klutz over there had been more careful like I told him, it wouldn't have run away. That poor baby gerbil will probably freeze to death or else starve over vacation. It's all your fault, Sidney Carlton. If you hadn't acted like such a sissy and been afraid of a helpless little gerbil, everything would have been just fine. . . ." Marcie went on and on telling the world what a louse and chicken I was.

How could this be my fault? Marcie was the stupid one, putting a crazy thing like a gerbil in that box. The class didn't think so, though. They just stared at me, especially A.J. Making a fool of me was his favorite sport. That gerbil knew what he was doing by running away. If only I could join it.

14
In the Driver's Seat

The first morning of vacation the phone rang. "Hello?" I answered.

"Satch? It's me, Spinner. Anything cooking today?"

"Naw. It's a slow day here, too, just waiting for Christmas to arrive."

"Any ideas?"

"You wanta go tobogganing?" I suggested.

"Sure, but I'll have to drag Frankie along, too. My mom's going bananas trying to keep him out of the presents."

"We-ell," I stalled. Frankie could spoil any good

time without even trying.

"How about asking Hai and Jao to go with us? That way Frankie and Jao could play together and not bug us."

I wasn't so sure about Hai. Ever since I'd gotten the short end of the snow shovel, things hadn't been the same between us. Spinner did have a point, though. Getting rid of Frankie took top priority.

"Yeah, OK," I said. "See you in ten minutes."

Adams Park was mobbed with kids. After pulling our gear up Cliffhanger's Run, the five of us climbed on board my toboggan. We had to show Hai and Jao what this was all about. I took the driver's seat. Jao and Hai sandwiched themselves in the middle. Frankie and Spinner brought up the rear.

"Now remember," I ordered, "lean the direction that I lean. That's how you steer this thing."

The slick snow made us fly down the hill like lightning. The toboggan was picking up so much speed, we were zipping by all kinds of sleds and snow saucers. Oh, oh. We were heading off course into the tree-lined hillsides! I leaned to the right, throwing as much body weight to the side as I could. The toboggan was still heading straight for timber.

"Lean right!" I screamed. My voice whizzed past my four passengers. "Lean, you turkeys. I can't turn this thing myself. We're gonna crash."

At last, someone back there started leaning. The toboggan swerved to the right, just in time. We missed the huge pine tree by inches, but we plowed right into some kids walking up the side of the hill. They were leveled by our toboggan, flat as a pancake.

Heads started to pop up out of the snow. A.J.'s face glared up at us. The fire coming out of his eyes melted the snow dripping from his cheeks. Right then and there I knew it was useless to try to explain the pileup.

"Hey, what's the big idea?" A.J. shouted. "You trying to kill somebody?"

"We're sorry, A.J.," I started. "We lost control."

"A sissy like you has no business in the driver's seat of a toboggan."

"It was an accident, A.J. These kids have never been on a—"

"*Aw,* can it, creep-o." A.J. didn't want explanations. He picked up a gob of snow and heaved it in Jao's face.

Jao started crying.

"How's that for an accident?" A.J. jeered.

Hai shook his fist at A.J. "No do again!"

"Hey, pick on somebody your own size," I yelled.

"I'm all for that," A.J. snapped.

He started toward me. For once I wasn't going to let A.J. get the best of me, even if it meant wearing two black eyes. Picking on a three-year-old was really the pits. A.J. leaped at me with a fist aimed dead center for my nose. I ducked and grabbed a handful of snow. Coming under A.J.'s swing, I mushed my snowy mitten right into his face. A.J. squirmed to get away. He no sooner wiped his face when I mushed another handful of cold snow against it.

A.J. backed away, stumbling for footing. This felt good. I started coming at A.J. with a third handful of snow. A.J. kept stepping back. He was turning chicken. Then A.J. broke into a run, and I tore out after him. I was in control. I was really in the driver's seat! Alex Jackson wasn't going to pick on Satch Carlton anymore. He wasn't going to get away with picking on Hai or Jao either. I would see to that!

A.J. was running across the field at top speed now, but I was closing in on him. He was going to learn his lesson, and I would be more than happy to teach it to him. In a few seconds he'd be boxed in. There was nowhere he could escape. The river had him cornered. A.J. wouldn't tangle with me again after he realized I wasn't afraid of him anymore.

A.J. reached the river. He wasn't slowing down. That fool. He was going to run across it. The river froze solid in February, sometimes even in January, but never in December.

"Come on, A.J., don't be stupid," I shouted.

A.J. looked back at me a second as if to consider what I'd said. Like a madman, he charged out onto the ice. *Crrrrack!* Down he sank! Oh, no! He could drown. Even A.J. didn't deserve that as a punishment.

"Help! Help!" A.J. cried.

"Don't panic!" I screamed. I guess I said it more for my own benefit than for A.J.'s. He couldn't possibly hear a word I said as he bobbed up and down in the icy water.

A log . . . a board . . . a branch. . . . I had to find something. But there was nothing, only white snow and ice everywhere. *Think, Satch—fast. A.J.'s drowning. Move!*

A.J.'s arms were grabbing furiously at pieces of

ice. His mouth and eyes opened and shut in terror. I couldn't watch any longer.

"Help!" A.J. yelled in desperation. The river's current ripped away at him, muffling his voice.

Pictures of ice rescues flashed through my mind. I was going to have to crawl out there on my stomach or have A.J.'s death on my conscience the rest of my life. I could fall through the ice, too.

I knelt down. I started to crawl out on the ice. I wasn't sure if the ice was juggling beneath me or if my insides were turning to Jell-O. I kept inching forward like an earthworm. A.J. still seemed miles and miles away. I tried to quicken my pace, but nothing seemed to help. I was still only halfway to him.

Huffing and puffing, Hai and Spinner arrived at the riverbank. "No, Satch, no! You'll go through, too. You'll both drown," Spinner screamed frantically.

"There's no other way. Go for help, Spinner," I yelled back, continuing to slither toward A.J.

Spinner didn't argue with me. He shot off for civilization.

Before I realized it, Hai was on his belly, too. His arms and legs were moving like a centipede. He could really travel.

"Hai, hold on to my legs when I reach A.J.," I ordered.

"OK," agreed Hai.

Somehow I didn't feel quite so alone, but I wondered if Hai would know what to do. After all, he'd never seen snow before this winter, let alone know what to do for an ice rescue.

The ice beneath me began to tremble. I could almost feel the current rushing underneath. *Please, God, don't let me fall through.* I crept forward. At last I reached the edge of the hole. Hai was behind me. I didn't want to put any weight down and crack the ice hole any larger. I stretched my body out for every inch it was worth. A.J. had gone crazy with fear. Though I was just inches away from his fingertips, he couldn't see me. I extended my arm out over the cold water as I stretched again. A.J.'s arms were flailing. I couldn't grab hold. I knew I'd have to edge out farther and risk going in, too.

"Hai, whatever happens, DON'T LET GO OF MY LEGS—NOT FOR ANYTHING!" I screamed.

I hoped he understood. He had to. Cautiously, I scooted my body forward. The ice shook. *Please, God, let the ice hold. I have to get closer.* I took a deep breath, and held it. I lunged over the water with the upper half of my body. I felt the ice giving way under my stomach. Into the water I sank. Hai squeezed like a tourniquet around my legs.

Finally, I could reach A.J. I wrapped my arms in a bear hug around his chest. Half of me was still submerged under water. I couldn't hold my breath any longer. The water was so cold it stung. Hai yanked on my legs, but A.J. and I weren't moving.

Pull, Hai. Pull, Hai. The current will take us away any minute. I don't want to drown. My lungs are gonna pop.

A.J. felt as heavy as a cement truck. By some miracle, Hai jerked enough to bob us out of the water. I grabbed a quick breath of air and went under again. Hai yanked again. My legs were three feet longer, but we gradually were coming out of that icy water.

Suddenly I realized A.J.'s body was limp. He was either dead or unconscious. I couldn't tell which as I tugged and tugged to pull him onto the ice. Every muscle I owned ached. I didn't want to let go of him, but the strength was oozing out of my body. My wet face had a layer of ice forming over it.

Hai tapped some hidden reserve of energy. He dragged the two of us across the ice, inch by inch. It seemed like forever, but we finally reached the riverbank. My frozen fingers almost cracked as I unwound them from A.J.'s body. Was he alive? I was too exhausted to find out. All I could do was lie flat on my back and pant.

Hai started pushing on A.J.'s stomach. Up and down. Up and down. A.J. still looked purple and lifeless. He wasn't breathing. Dizzy and sapped of all but enough strength to breathe myself, I crawled over to help Hai.

I rolled A.J. on his side and slugged the middle of his back. Water streamed out of his mouth. We turned him onto his back again. I grabbed his mouth and started blowing into it. I remembered seeing mouth-to-mouth resuscitation in health class, but I never paid very close attention. I never thought I'd have to use it. I kept blowing air into his lungs and gasping for air myself. Blow and gasp. Blow and gasp. Over and over. Was he alive? Would this help?

"Come on, A.J., breathe."

Blow. Gasp. Blow. Gasp.

Finally A.J. started coughing. Really coughing. "He's alive!" Hai and I sat A.J. up and patted his back. A.J. gasped for air. He was still out of it. All I could see were the whites of his eyes. His eyeballs were hidden somewhere up in his forehead. *Oh, God, help.*

A.J.'s body started to shiver. His teeth shook. His shoulders shook. His legs shook. His whole body rattled. Hai took off his dry jacket and wrapped it around A.J.'s quivering body. A.J. was totally blue now, even his lips.

Hai and I started to shiver, too. In the struggle to save A.J., we had forgotten how cold we were.

In the background, I could hear a siren growing louder. Spinner was running down the hill toward us. Frankie and Jao were close behind. Hai and I looked at each other in silence. *Thanks, God.* We'd done it. We'd rescued A.J.

15
Growing Up,
Not Down

"Will he make it?" I begged the ambulance driver. "Will he? Will he?" I had to hear it over and over just to be sure.

"He's going to pull through. Don't worry, boys. We'll take over from here. You did great." They loaded A.J. onto the stretcher and into the ambulance.

"Hey, fellas," called an attendant, "climb aboard. The doctors will want to make sure you're OK, too. You look like you've had a pretty rough time of it yourselves."

He was right. I was still shivering, but it didn't

seem important until A.J. was safe.

Hai and I crawled into the ambulance. Spinner took Frankie and Jao home. I've always pictured an ambulance ride as something really cool—riding around town with the sirens blaring. Somehow, it didn't seem so cool now.

People in white mobbed us at the hospital. A.J. was whisked away on a cart they put under his stretcher. He still only looked half alive. A nurse led Hai and me to an examination room.

"The doctor will be here in a few minutes. He's attending your friend first." She stuck thermometers in our mouths and left.

At last Hai and I took a deep breath in unison.

"You OK, Satch?" Hai mumbled between the thermometer and his tongue.

"Yeah. Thanks, pal. You saved us." I sniffed.

Hai looked upward. "Had help, Satch."

I knew what he meant.

"I think maybe you both die. This no good." Hai's eyes were tearing up. So were mine. We hugged each other.

Mom came running in the room. As soon as she saw me, she burst into tears. "Satch," she sobbed, "thank God you're alive." She hugged me and kissed me hysterically. Three times she stopped a little. Then she cried again and went back to squeezing me. Finally collecting herself, she gave Hai a big squeeze, too.

"What happened, Satch?" Mom gasped. "All Spinner told me after he called the ambulance was that A.J. had gone through the ice, and you and Hai were trying to save him. We thought you'd all drown."

"Well, that pretty much covers it. The whole thing happened so fast. There wasn't time for anything else."

Mom hugged me again, just to make sure I was alive after all. "Didn't you know you were all apt to drown?"

"Yeah, Mom, but. . . ." My mind flashed back to the endless minutes I spent crawling on the ice. I'd felt like I was dragging lead weights. I could see A.J.'s helpless arms flailing wildly in the air. I shivered remembering my lungs about to pop and thinking I was about to die. In slow motion I saw myself wrap my arms around A.J. knowing no matter what, I couldn't let go. "But, Mom, I had to. I just had to. A.J. was going to die. I couldn't live with myself if I'd stood there and done nothing."

"I know, Satch. That's the kind of person you are. I'm proud of you. It's just that I was so scared of losing you, the way you were afraid of losing A.J." Mom started crying again. I hugged her extra tight.

In a while the doctor came in and examined Hai and me. "You're very brave young men and very lucky, too," the doctor said. "Alex is going to come through. He must be one special friend to have you two risk your lives for him."

Special. *Hmm.* Complicated was more like it.

After Mom dropped Hai off at his house, she headed the car home. She was still pretty jittery. Her voice cracked a little as she tried to hold back more tears. "You know, Satch, sometimes I treat you like a child. Mothers don't like to admit their children grow up. Maybe it makes us feel older. Maybe it makes us feel unneeded. I don't exactly know why. But we all do it. I guess I just want you to know, Satch, I'll try to remember that you've become a man. You've certainly proven that today."

I didn't know what to say. Mom, calling me a man. I could hardly believe my ears. At long last, I was growing up instead of down.

The next day was Christmas Eve. Our tree had been sitting in the garage for two weeks. We always decorated it at night on Christmas Eve. Then the presents would miraculously appear under it Christmas morning.

"Satch, what do you think about inviting the Lings over tonight to help trim the tree?" Mom asked. "Hai and his family might enjoy it. I'm sure they've never experienced this custom before."

"Yeah, I guess so," I answered. Then I began to wonder. "Mom, I don't think the Ling family celebrates Christmas."

"You're right, Satch, but we won't turn it into a formal affair. Our faith teaches love and understanding. Our example will be only to share that, not to make them change their customs or beliefs."

I remember Reverend Miller had said something like that. I guess the Ling family wasn't brought to America on the condition that they go to our church. The churches helped them because love and caring was what we were about.

Mom was smarter than I ever realized.

16
The Missing Pieces

The Lings arrived at 6:30. "Goot evening. How are you today?" Mr. Ling greeted my mother. He bowed. She bowed.

"Goot evening, How are you today?" Mr. Ling greeted Carrie. He bowed. She bowed.

Mr. Ling headed my way. I knew what was coming. I bowed.

Mrs. Ling entered. She went through the same procedure. Then Grandmother appeared. She shortened her entrance to a simple bow. The kids streamed in and we all bowed. Hai slapped my hand, American style, when he reached me. I'd taught him something.

Hai and I took off for the living room where the empty Christmas tree stood along with the goodies Mom had set out. We dove into the cookies.

The rest of the family filed into the room. They smiled a lot, but sat stiff and erect on the sofa. Even Hai seemed a little nervous.

Mom tried to look calm. She passed around the fudge and said, "Satch, would you start unwrapping the ornaments while I hang the lights on the tree? Maybe Hai would like to help you."

Hai unwrapped a wood train painted brightly with red lacquer. The little bell inside even jingled. The whole thing was only about two inches long and was extremely intricate. Hai tenderly inspected it. He smiled. He turned the train over to look at the underside. Suddenly his eyes lit up. He chattered something in Vietnamese to his family. The whole family leaned forward. All kinds of chattering went on in Vietnamese as they passed the little red train back and forth. Everyone who held the train grinned excitedly.

"What is it, Hai? Are you looking at the year? What's so fascinating?" Curiosity was gnawing away at me.

Hai held up the ornament. "See here, Satch," he said, pointing to the bottom of the train.

I squinted to see what he was talking about. "All it says is 1980. That's the year it was made."

"No, Satch, look closer. There's more."

I moved in for a closer look and read: Made in Hong Kong. "So? That just means it was made there and sold in one of the stores here."

"You right, but there is more. Look at the *H* in Hong Kong."

I squinted some more. "It looks just like an *H* to me."

"It is *my H*. My *H* for Hai. *I* make this train in Hong Kong. I put a special little double bar across it. *I* make this train," Hai announced.

"You? Really? When? How?" A million questions needed answering. "But you were in Vietnam, not Hong Kong."

"In 1978 we leave Vietnam. Army from north coming. Kill my country's people. Make slaves of others. No stay. Must escape. In night, we leave. Cost much money. Buy trip on boat. Boat take my family in ocean."

"Where did you go? What was it like?"

"Take ten days. Boat take 183 people. Sixty, my family. All my aunt and uncle, cousin. Boat like size of . . .," Hai searched for a comparison, "like size of two of this room."

Wow! That was small for 183 people. "How did you move? How did you sleep for ten days? How did you eat? Wasn't it terrible?"

"Sleep, take turns. Eat, fish in ocean."

"Weren't you scared all people would make that small boat sink? You could have drowned!"

"No think to be frightened. Must do. Army worse. Army kill. Must do. Must do. Boat only chance."

In my mind I saw all those refugee pictures again. Suddenly, Hai's face was there in the middle of the picture. His clothes were tattered. His bones stuck out from his face. He was one of those people who had nothing left except his life.

"Is Hong Kong where your boat landed?"

"No, we turned away from many islands. We sit in Hong Kong on boat many, many day. Grandfather die there. Mai very sick. Finally, we get to come on land. Live long years in Hong Kong."

"Years? What happened?"

"We wait. That is all we can do."

"Wait for what?"

"Wait for home. Wait for country. That is why we so thankful now to have home. America. You do not know how life is without country. Without home. You no fighting. You no hunger."

"Where is the rest of your family now? I mean your cousins and aunts and uncles?" Lisa asked.

"Some in California. Some in Ohio. Some still in Hong Kong waiting. We all work to save money. Even I work shoveling snow. Money will help bring family to America. Home."

So that's why Hai was such an energetic snow shoveler. He needed that money for his family. The pieces of the puzzle finally fit together. Hai desperately needed money. Somehow, that dirt bike seemed pretty unimportant.

Questions kept leaping out of Carrie and Lisa now. Even Mom looked curious, but she was too polite to pry.

"Where did you live in Hong Kong? How did you have money for food and clothes? Vietnamese money wouldn't be any good, would it? What language do they speak in Hong Kong?"

The Ling family tried to answer questions. Mr. and

Mrs. Ling couldn't keep up with them all. Mostly, the kids answered.

"I sew," Hai's oldest sister announced.

"I cook," Mrs. Ling stated.

"Father work in factory. Sisters and me work in factory. I make these." Hai smiled and held up the tiny red train again.

"House dirt floor. All sleep in two beds. Beds on floor. Mats. No water," Hai's other sister explained.

Mrs. Ling spoke up. "America happy. America home. Everyone smile in America."

Mrs. Ling didn't have to speak perfect English to get her message across. Her face said it for her.

In no time at all, everyone started hanging ornaments. Each time an ornament was unwrapped, we inspected it carefully for Hai's special H in Hong Kong. We didn't find any more, but one was all we needed to make this night special.

About eight o'clock the doorbell rang. It was the Jacksons.

"Hello," Mom said, startled to see them. "Please come in."

Mr. and Mrs. Jackson cautiously stepped into the living room. A.J. wasn't with them. They looked surprised to see the Lings. Oh, no. Had they come to chew me out for chasing A.J. onto the ice? What had A.J. told them?

"We hate to interrupt your Christmas Eve, but we just felt compelled to stop by and personally thank Satch and Hai." Mr. Jackson's voice started to crack. "A.J. wouldn't be alive today if you boys hadn't risked your own lives to save his."

Mrs. Jackson continued softly, "We can't tell you how much this means to us." Her eyes filled with tears.

"It's OK. Anyone would have done it," I said, trying to comfort Mrs. Jackson. Maybe that wasn't exactly true, but I didn't want to sound like a hot-shot hero. "How's A.J. doing?"

"The doctors say they'll release him tomorrow morning. It will be the best Christmas present we could have asked for." Mr. Jackson shifted his hat from hand to hand, fumbling for words. "I guess I just don't know how to express our gratitude."

The Jacksons turned to go. Mr. Jackson started to put his hat back on, and then at the last moment he turned to Hai and me. "You know, we've already lost one son. I just don't think we could have lived through losing A.J., too."

Mrs. Jackson started to sniffle. My mother patted her on the back and walked her to the door. The Lings filed out behind the Jacksons, all bowing as they reached the doorway.

Lost one son already? I didn't know anything had happened to A.J.'s brother.

"Mom, did A.J.'s brother run away from home or something?"

"No, not that I know of."

"What did Mr. Jackson mean about losing a son?"

"Mr. Jackson wasn't talking about A.J.'s brother in high school. He was talking about A.J.'s older brother, John. John would probably be about thirty. He's an MIA."

"MIA? What's that?"

"It means missing in action," Mom explained. "A.J.'s brother was in the Vietnam War. He flew a bomber. During a mission, his plane was shot down. A.J.'s brother parachuted out. No one knows if he was killed or captured. The Army just reports him as MIA or missing in action."

"But, Mom, the war's been over for years. Wouldn't he be released if he had been a prisoner?"

"Well, in most wars that happens, but it hasn't happened in this war. The families of many soldiers still have no idea whether their sons were killed or are still being starved and tortured in prison camps. It's not a pleasant thought. You can imagine what grief the Jacksons live with."

"How come we never heard any of this in school?"

"Well, most of the Vietnam War history isn't in books yet. It's a war most Americans would just as soon forget. Some Americans probably aren't even aware that prisoners may still be in Vietnam. To the families of MIAs, the war will never end until they have the truth about their sons. Even if the Jacksons knew John had died, they could at least put their minds to rest."

"But, Mom, after all this time, don't you think his chances of being alive are pretty slim?"

"True, Satch, it doesn't look good for John. Putting it out of your mind is a lot trickier than that, though. Remember A.J. in the river?"

"Yeah?"

"How would you feel if your last sight of A.J. was seeing him struggle? What if you never knew what happened? What if you had to live with that as a final memory? Wouldn't it haunt you?"

"I see what you mean." My mind was whizzing through that horrible moment. It was like some ghastly video on constant replay.

Mom put her arm around me and looked down at me. "I doubt there's a day that goes by, it doesn't break their hearts." She started to get teary eyed. "Now do you understand how painful it would have been for them to lose A.J., too?"

"Yeah. I never knew about A.J.'s brother before. It explains a lot of things between A.J. and Hai."

"Are there problems?" Mom looked worried.

"Not anymore. I'll take care of them." I kissed Mom good night and hurried upstairs.

17
Tomorrow

Even though today was Christmas, I felt different than I usually do on present-opening day. It had always seemed so exciting before. But today I kept thinking about A.J. I knew he was OK as far as living and breathing. But his crazy way of acting tough really bothered me. Was he blaming Hai for taking away his brother John? Had this accident shown him Hai wasn't an enemy after all? Could he return to the old A.J.? I had to know.

Dad arrived to pick up us kids for Christmas evening with him. "Satch, are you in one piece now?"

"Yeah."

"You sounded kinda shaky on the phone the other night. I'm really proud of you. I always knew you had a good head on those shoulders. To tell the truth, Satch, I'm not sure I would have been able to keep my wits about me. You really are someone special."

"Thanks, Dad." I half smiled. I liked Dad thinking I was a great kid, but I didn't like the feeling of saving A.J. so I could become a hero. That wasn't why I did it.

Dad looked me straight in the eye. "Something's still bothering you, isn't it, Sport?"

"Sort of."

"Wanta talk?"

"I guess so."

"Is it still A.J.?"

"How'd you know?"

"Just a hunch. I remember you talking about A.J. and Hai being at odds. Is it still a problem?"

"More than ever." My thoughts started escaping. "Dad, did you know A.J. has an older brother who's an MIA in Vietnam?"

"I'd forgotten all about that. It seems so long ago."

"I guess it's not so long ago for the Jacksons. I think A.J. has been taking things out on Hai because he's from Vietnam. That's how this whole mess of falling through the ice started."

Dad sounded serious, "Well, Satch, you probably have something there. That would certainly explain A.J.'s attitude. The question now, Satch, is what do you want to do about it?"

"I don't know, Dad. I guess that's what's really buggin' me."

Dad put his arm on my shoulder. He bent down and looked me squarely in the eye, "Satch, God didn't save you and your friends out there on that ice for nothing. He had a reason."

Hmm. God had a reason. He didn't save us for nothing. . . . "Dad, do you think you could drive me and Hai over to A.J.'s? We won't stay long. But I gotta go. We gotta settle this."

Dad didn't need any persuasion.

I called Mrs. Jackson first. She was delighted. "Satch, that's a marvelous idea. A.J.'s kind of down in the dumps. Your visit is the perfect medicine."

I called Hai next. "Hai, I've got the answer."

"What answer? What you talk about?"

"A.J. Now I know why he's been so rotten." I explained about A.J.'s brother.

"I see," Hai said. I could almost hear his head bobbing up and down.

"Do you want to go over to A.J.'s? Maybe we can straighten out this whole mixed-up mess."

"Yes, Satch. We go. We take care problem. I know war. I know A.J. feeling. We fix, Satch. You and me."

"Right, Hai. You and me."

Dad and I picked up Hai and headed across town. Hai and I didn't have a plan, but we were on the same wavelength. We knew we had to try together.

The car stopped in A.J.'s drive. "I'll wait out here. Good luck," Dad winked.

Mrs. Jackson led Hai and me into the family room. A.J. was on the couch surrounded by a mountain of food, books, and pillows. His face was still swollen, but back to its normal color. His eyes cautiously watched us as we entered.

Nervously, I searched for words. I wasn't sure yet if A.J. wanted to thank me for saving his life or punch me out for chasing him onto the ice.

"Hi, A.J. How ya feeling?" I tried to sound friendly, like nothing had happened.

"Hi," A.J. mumbled. "Come on in." His voice was only half there.

"You be OK?" Hai asked, coming forward.

"Yeah," A.J. looked down. I sensed he wanted to say more but couldn't get it out.

"You be back to school?" Hai was trying to keep the conversation going.

"Yeah. . . . Doc says a few days in bed will do it."

None of us knew what to say. Finally, I had to say it. "A.J., I'm sorry. I never meant for it to come to this; I never wanted you to die. It's gone too far. We've got to end this."

"You don't have anything to be sorry about. I'm the one who's been a first class-jerk." A.J. buried his face in his hands. I think he was crying. Bravely, he lifted his head and whispered, "I'm sorry."

Now his words came more rapidly, "Thanks, guys. I guess I owe you my life. I was crazy to run out on that thin ice. I guess I've been doing a lot of crazy things lately."

My voice quavered, "It's OK, A.J. We're all here now. We can work it out."

A.J. started to pour everything out. "All I remember after I fell through the ice was knowing I was gonna die." He took a breath. "I didn't want to die. I couldn't let my parents down. They would absolutely fall apart. They couldn't bear it, not after losing John."

A.J. finally glanced up at Hai. "You see, Hai, I had you all confused with my brother, John. Looking at you made me think about him. We still don't know if John is dead or alive in Vietnam. I used to block it out of my mind, but then you moved here. I had to think about it all the time."

"We know about your brother. You don't have to explain, A.J." I tried to assure him.

"I thought blaming Hai would make it better. It didn't. It just made the pain worse."

Hai spoke up, "OK, A.J. OK now. I know this pain. War bring much hate. War no good, anyone. War not just kill people dead. War eat at person inside."

A.J. looked up at Hai, as if he just realized that Hai had been scarred by war, too.

Hai pointed to his chest. "War inside much worse. Not go away. I know hurt. It never disappear. I see family kill. Some family torture. Some family still not escape. But, A.J., we hope. Hope all we have. Hope help pain in mind get better. My Cwizmas present to you, A.J., give you hope."

Wow! I always knew Hai had a computer for a brain, but I'd underestimated him. Hai was something extraordinary. In all his pain, in all his suffering, in all that he had endured, Hai could *forgive.*

A.J. reached out and gave Hai a weak high five. We all laughed.

Hai and I climbed into the car beside Dad.

"Everything work out?"

"Yep. You were right, Dad."

Dad kidded, "Who me? Your old dad, right?"

I smiled at Dad. He understood.

We dropped Hai off at his house. I called out the door after him, "Hey, it's supposed to snow tomorrow. Wanta shovel together?"

"Sure. Call me." Hai waved and disappeared inside.

"Dad," I turned to explain, "A.J. was really hurting inside. So was Hai. We straightened it out. We understand each other now."

"Sometimes even adults never manage that, Satch, even though it sounds so simple. You've really grown up. I couldn't be prouder of you." Dad tossled my hair like the old days.

The Christmas lights shone all down Oliver Street. The last three days still spun around in my mind. So much had happened. It seemed almost like three years. Mom and Dad actually thought I was grown up.

Christmas never felt so good before.

SATCH AND THE MOTORMOUTH

Sixth grade's terrific!

Everyone likes Satch—including Miss Hepburn, the neatest teacher at Roosevelt School, who even makes spelling rules fun!

Satch only has one problem—Motormouth Marcie Cook. How can one girl be so loud and obnoxious? Of all the kids in class, why does she sit behind him? Why do they always end up having to work together—at church as well as at school? And he's pretty sure Marcie's responsible for the anonymous valentines he's getting.

Nothing could be worse! Or could it?

What about being covered with itchy chicken pox?

Or getting caught in a hailstorm of eggs?

Or a *silent* Marcie?

Read about Satch and the gang
in these exciting books!

New Kid on the Block
Satch and the Motormouth

KAREN SOMMER teaches third graders and has twin boys of her own. Her writing career began when her students begged for more of the stories she composed for class. She's been writing ever since!